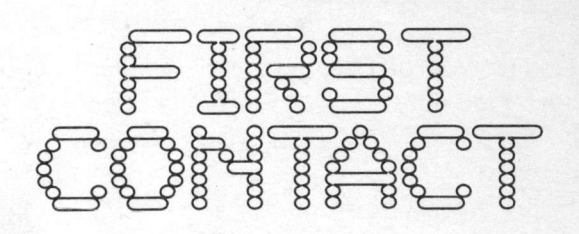

FIRST CONTACT

And then the ship – for that is what the egg-shape was – began to move again, slowly increasing its speed until it was little more than a blur in the interstellar night. It had found and identified its destination and now it was vital to reach it with all speed, to reach that insignificant yellow star and its planets.

And one planet in particular; a planet which, long ago when the ship had started on its mission, had been a tiny blue world teeming with countless different forms of life. A planet which was now all but dead and deserted.

A planet which had once been known as Earth.

Also in the Point SF series:

Obernewtyn – The Obernewtyn Chronicles,
  Book One
The Farseekers – The Obernewtyn Chronicles,
  Book Two
Isobelle Carmody

Random Factor
Jessica Palmer

Look out for:

Virus
Molly Brown

Soul Snatchers
Stan Nicholls

First Contact II
Nigel Robinson

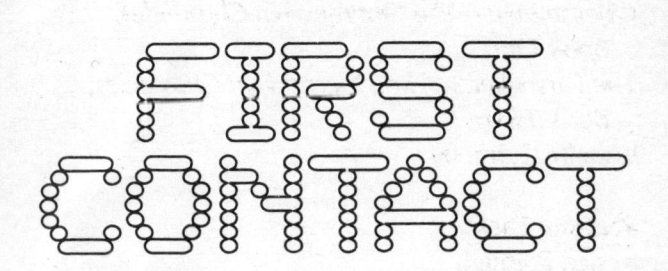

Nigel Robinson

SCHOLASTIC

Scholastic Children's Books,
Scholastic Publications Ltd,
7–9 Pratt Street, London NW1 0AE, UK

Scholastic Inc.,
555 Broadway, New York, NY 10012-3999, USA

Scholastic Canada Ltd,
123 Newkirk Road, Richmond Hill, Ontario, Canada L4C 3G5

Ashton Scholastic Pty Ltd,
PO Box 579, Gosford, New South Wales, Australia

Ashton Scholastic Ltd,
Private Bag 92801, Penrose, Auckland, New Zealand

First published in the UK
by Scholastic Publications Ltd, 1994

Text copyright © Nigel Robinson, 1994

ISBN 0 590 55493 X

Typeset by DP Photosetting, Aylesbury, Bucks
Printed by Cox & Wyman Ltd, Reading, Berks

10 9 8 7 6 5 4 3 2 1

CONTENTS

Part Three – The Seti

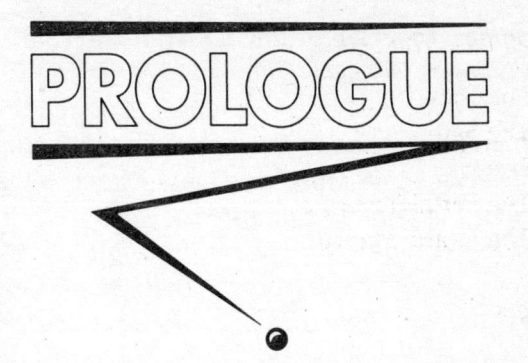

PROLOGUE

Down through the centuries the EarthLifers have always regarded Man as the pinnacle of creation, and all other creatures as subservient to him. Their new charismatic leader, Donovan Trueheart, has certainly been riding a massive wave of support on all twenty-one worlds in the System, as well as TerraNova itself.

However, while of course not disputing claims of the System's Security Overlord, it's perhaps salutary to realize that other former terran species have also displayed some impressive levels of intelligence.

Until their extinction in the early twenty-third century, the dolphins, an aquatic mammal, displayed a sophisticated social network, and high levels of reasoning. They were able to communicate with each other as well as with human beings.

And we must also consider the dinosaurs. Our common conception of these giant lizards, gathered mainly from fossils found on Home Planet, is that of ferocious but bumbling monsters.

On the contrary, they were the most successful species ever to inhabit Home Planet. Homo sapiens has existed for a little under six thousand years. The dinosaurs, on the other hand, ruled our former home planet for over two hundred million years, before they were all mysteriously wiped out sixty-five million years ago.

To this day we still do not know exactly what killed the dinosaurs, and the reason behind their demise remains one of science's greatest mysteries. But one thing seems certain: the dinosaurs were the biggest threat to the small burrowing mammals which inhabited the planet at that time. With the dinosaurs gone, these mammals were able to evolve in relative security, into the Highest Mammal of them all – Man himself.

If the dinosaurs were still alive today it's highly unlikely that Mankind would be around to see them.

– Extract from the *Encyclopaedia Systematica*, Amalthean University Press, AD3243

INTERLUDE

Nine Years to Earth

In the ice-black space between the stars the huge object slowly came to a silent halt and hung, suspended in the fathomless, all-encompassing void. If there had been human eyes to watch they would have said that it looked like nothing less than a giant egg, apart from the fact that its dull gun-metal-grey hull was studded with the impact marks of innumerable meteoroid storms encountered in its two-thousand years journey.

Unexpectedly the craft began to turn on its axis. And with that seemingly insignificant but purposeful movement the egg-shape suddenly gained a new meaning. No longer could it be dismissed as just another piece of space detritus, perhaps flung out from an interstellar explosion many millions of years ago.

Now it was an artefact, a *tool*, made and fashioned by thinking hands. Indeed, the egg-shape itself seemed to possess an intelligence of its own: as it spun around it was almost as if it were surveying the myriad stars which blazed white and steady in the all-encompassing and fathomless void. Checking and re-checking. Evaluating and then discarding. Listening to the pulse of the Universe.

Searching for one particular star.

Then it jarred to a halt. An almost imperceptible shudder ran through it, and along the length of its hull rows of countless tiny lights flared up, as the object shook itself out of its two-thousand-year torpor. It had found what it had been searching for, the one star amidst the millions in this galaxy.

A small, insignificant yellow star.

Within the hollowed-out interior of the egg-shape the temperature rose dramatically; in the space of a few hours the stale, dead and musty atmosphere had been replaced by the tart and biting tang of a mixture of methane and ammonia, and the air was suddenly filled with a strange tinkling and whirring noise, like the sound of a thousand pieces of sophisticated equipment suddenly sparking once more into action.

And *things* began to move inside the egg-shape, things which had been sleeping for a long, long time, like creatures awakening from a centuries-long deep hibernation. At first these creatures moved sluggishly as they experienced difficulties in readjusting to their familiar environment, then they started to move more sharply and purposefully. An excited chittering and chirruping arose inside the egg-shape, and awareness once more dawned on the creatures who had just woken from their seemingly endless sleep. Once again they remembered who they were, and what their great purpose was. Once again they remembered the shocking discovery their astronomers and philosophers had made long centuries ago when they were scanning the heavens and listening in to the music of the spheres with their radio telescopes.

And then the ship – for that is what the egg-shape was – began to move again, slowly increasing its speed until it was little more than a blur in the interstellar night. It had found and identified its destination and now it was vital to reach it with all speed, to reach that insignificant yellow star and its planets.

And one planet in particular; a planet which, long ago when the ship had started on its mission, had been a tiny blue world teeming with countless different forms of life. A planet which was now all but dead and deserted.

A planet which had once been known as Earth.

Late-night news broadcast from WNN (World News Network): 21 July 2169.

And finally ... The historians amongst you might recall the so-called Search for ExtraTerrestrial Intelligences. Established in the late twentieth century, this project was designed to search the Universe for any signs of life, intelligent or otherwise.

For two centuries now the heavens have remained obstinately silent. At least until now, that is. According to reports just in from the prestigious Hawking Research Institute there is, after all, someone out there.

HRI director, Professor Barbara Jenner, has announced that for the past two years her team has been detecting a radio source in the area of the star Van Biesbroeck. The regular, apparently artificial, nature of the emissions strongly suggests the presence of an alien intelligence, Professor Jenner said in a press conference today.

EarthLife, however, the environmental and religious fringe group, have strongly criticized the report. Coming as it does on the two-hundredth anniversary of Man's first landing on the Moon, a spokesperson described the report as a cheap publicity stunt by the HRI in its campaign for the establishment of a permanent research base on Mars. Professor Jenner described the accusations as "typical of antediluvian thinkers who would have us believe that the Earth is still flat".

According to the Professor, the Van Biesbroeck star is over twenty light years away from the Earth. Even if the alleged "aliens" could travel at a fraction of the speed of light it would take them thousands of years to reach Earth. Such a speed is quite clearly impossible, said Professor Jenner.

So, viewers, it looks as though you can all sleep soundly in your beds tonight. It doesn't seem as if we'll be expecting little green men on our doorsteps tomorrow morning, or any other morning for that matter.

And on that welcome note, that's the end of today's programming on WNN. Oxygen levels are still low, so remember to adjust your compensators before turning in for the night. You're also reminded that from midnight the new meat rationing law for Western Europe comes into force; any violation of the new strictures will, of course, be met with the appropriate action.

And that's all, fellow citizens. Have a peaceful and plague-free sleep...

The seventeen-year-old girl clicked off the video and sighed. She looked around at her six companions, who had been sitting hunched around the video set in the small room for about an hour now. There was a look of disbelief on their young and innocent faces.

"That was a news broadcast made in 2169, one thousand and seventy-four years ago, by the World News Network," she explained. "It was only by pure chance that I came across it, hidden away in the Academy library."

"Well, it was successful then, wasn't it, Marla?" said one of her colleagues, a gauche-looking boy only a couple of years younger than her.

"What d'you mean, Corin?" asked Marla.

"The Research Institute got their base on Mars, after all," Corin continued. "Their publicity stunt worked."

"That's right," agreed another of the students gathered there. "If not for the success of that first base we probably wouldn't have colonized Mars in the first place and there wouldn't be a TerraNova we could call home!"

"It's not your home, Anya," Corin pointed out rather pedantically. "You were born here on Pasiphae like the rest of us."

"What was Western Europe though?" asked another. "I seem to remember reading about it on a vid-disk once."

Marla gritted her teeth. "Don't you get the point?" she asked patiently. Five blank faces stared at her; only one head nodded in understanding. *Godammit!* she cursed. *Am I dealing with children here or what*?

"Earth scanners—" she began but was interrupted by Corin.

"You shouldn't use that name any more," he said. "Its official name is Home Planet now ... that's what we're supposed to call it."

Marla breathed deeply, in an effort to control her temper. She caught the eye of the one person who had nodded. Unlike the others here, he was a year older than her; to her infuriation he was chuckling at their companions' formality. She glared daggers at him: they had been together for almost a year now and he still delighted in mocking her earnestness.

"OK, the Home Planet's scanners picked up on something way back in the twenty-second century," she said. "An artificial intelligence..."

"A publicity stunt," said Corin. "A successful publicity stunt, I'll give you that, but a publicity stunt all the same."

"Since when do publicity stunts move faster than the speed of light then?" she asked pointedly.

"That's impossible," Corin said. "Nothing can move faster than the speed of light. Hawking physics categorically state that..."

"Well, something is," Marla said. "That signal the scientists of the twenty-second century picked up has been getting nearer and nearer to us every century."

"Have you got any evidence?" Corin asked.

Marla looked over to the swarthy good-looking eighteen-year-old who had chuckled. "Cruse?"

Cruse stepped forward and threw several computer disks down onto the desk at which Marla was sitting.

"These are taken from official System records," he announced, and a buzz of interest ran through the tiny room. Cruse moved over to Marla's side and she automatically put her arm around his waist.

"System records?" gasped Corin, and added automatically: "But that's illegal..."

"So is meeting here in secret," said Cruse.

"Are you sure that we're safe?" Anya asked nervously.

Cruse nodded. "The room's been scanned for bugs," he said, "and there's a ServoRobot on guard outside. We can talk freely."

Corin fingered the disks, and gazed enquiringly at them, as if trying to tease out from them the electronic information that they held. "So what do these disks say?" he asked.

"That the System has been monitoring the progress of this 'intelligence' over the centuries," Cruse replied.

"I can't believe that," said Anya. "How could you have accessed that knowledge, Cruse?"

"I've been a top-A physics student at the Academy," Cruse reminded her. "My teacher, Jarrl, gave me special clearance to access the Academy's info-files whenever I want." He picked up a disk, and fingered it almost lovingly. "Of course, this isn't the sort of information he thought I'd come across..."

"But why haven't we been told about any of this?" asked Corin.

Marla laughed bitterly. "Why haven't you been told what really happened to your parents when they went 'missing', Corin?" she asked, and the younger boy fell silent, as Marla turned to the girls. "Or you, Anya. You're one of our best biochemists. But will they let you travel off-world to study the methane swamps of Jupiter?"

Anya shook her head.

"I last saw my parents three years ago," Marla said. "Like Anya's they were biochemists. But my parents were also given clearance to travel often to Earth – I mean, the Home Planet. The last time I saw them they seemed worried, as if they had discovered something ... something they shouldn't have. I never saw them again. A System official told me later that they had died in a space shuttle accident."

"I'm sorry ..." said Anya.

"I hacked into Spaceport records," said Marla, and looked up at Cruse. "With the help of Cruse's computer skills. There were no space shuttle accidents that day ... there weren't even any flights that day. The System had lied to me."

"But that's unthinkable," said Corin. "The System is here to protect us all."

"'The System provides and I am content'," mocked Cruse, repeating the creed that every young Academician was required to learn upon starting school.

"We're all meeting here in secret because we

suspect that there's something wrong with the way we are governed," said Marla.

"Are you sure we're safe?" Corin asked again anxiously.

"I told you," Cruse said irritably. "There's a ServoRobot guarding the door. No one will be able to get past it."

"We're here because we want to demand a say in the way we're governed," said Marla. "We're Academicians, the *crème de la crème*. In a few years we will all have graduated, and will be appointed to positions of power."

"Then let's make our demands when we've graduated," said Anya, who was uncertain of Marla's schemes.

"When you've become a part of the System? When you're part of the establishment?" scoffed Cruse. "We're watched almost every hour of the day already – it'll be even worse then! We must attack the System now, from the outside, not try and destabilize it later from within."

"That's right," said Marla eagerly. "We want to be able to travel to the other planets, and if not we want to know why. We want to have a voice in our future, and not have it decided for us by some faceless computer or bureaucrat. We want to know what's happening on Earth—"

"Home Planet," Cruse reminded her, with irony in his voice.

"Nothing's happening on Home Planet," protested Corin. "It's a wasteland now, everyone knows that."

Cruse glanced down at the disks on the desk, and shook his head. "That's not what those disks say," he claimed. "There are things on them that . . . that don't add up. . ."

"Such as?" Corin wasn't convinced.

"Huge consignments of trans-uranic elements mined on Jupiter or Saturn, for instance," he said. "They're taken off-world but they're never delivered anywhere – not to TerraNova, nor the Asteroid Belt. They must be taken somewhere."

"You think that they've been taken to Earth – I mean Home Planet?" asked Anya.

Cruse shrugged, and indicated another disk.

"That contains a copy of the census returns for the twenty-one worlds of the System," he explained. "There are discrepancies on that disk too, figures which don't tally. People are going missing, Anya. . ."

Anya frowned. She had heard many similar rumours in the past; indeed over the years several of her fellow students at the Academy had one day simply not turned up for class and had never been seen again. But to voice suspicions could be regarded as treason. It was said that Donovan Trueheart's spies were everywhere, just waiting to bring to justice anyone who might be thought capable of fomenting unrest against the all-powerful System.

"What are you saying, Cruse?" she asked, even though she already knew the answer.

"That the System is corrupt," he said. "That it's hiding vital facts from us, Anya. That it's probably even killing off those who don't agree with its policies and politics..."

"No, I can't believe that!" she said. "The System is there for our benefit. At least we're now at peace and there's no starvation or disease – remember the history books, Cruse. Do you remember reading about the bad days of the 24th century? Billions of people were wiped out by disease and the love plague, and war and famine. You wouldn't want to go back to those days, would you?"

Cruse looked steadily at the young girl. "I'd like the freedom to make up my own mind," he said. "And if you look into yourself, if you ask yourself what really happened to your parents, I think so would you."

Anya lowered her eyes. She knew that Cruse was right: why else would she have agreed to come to this meeting in the first place if she hadn't had her own doubts about the System?

"We're only six people," she said. "What can we do?"

"There must be more like us all over Pasiphae," said Cruse.

"Yes, criminals and vagrants in the Wastelands," sneered Corin. "Ne'er-do-wells who are too insignificant for the System even to bother about."

Cruse ignored him. "And there are probably even more on the other planets." His dark eyes gleamed with youthful enthusiasm. "We're young, we're the future of the System. Let's show them what we're capable of! We demand freedom and free speech and free thought for all!"

"A very pretty speech indeed," boomed a voice behind them. They all turned around.

"Lord Trueheart!" gasped Marla, and stood up to welcome the fabled Security Chief of the whole System itself. Trueheart brushed aside her proffered hand of welcome.

"It's certainly an honour to see you here on Pasiphae, sir," said Anya, and looked warily past the great man to the black-uniformed and jack-booted guards in the open doorway behind him.

Donovan Trueheart yawned theatrically and stalked around the tiny room, as six pairs of eyes followed him, none more suspicious or hating than Cruse's.

"Let us say I was passing by," he said with affected nonchalance. "It's Graduation Day for you soon, isn't it, Marla?" he asked.

"Why yes, sir," she said. "I'm surprised you know my name."

Trueheart stopped, and looked her firmly in the eyes. "I know many things, Marla," he said pointedly, and turned to Cruse. "Let us say that I am the guest of honour at the Graduation Ceremony."

"That's indeed a great honour for us all, sir," Cruse said, trying hard to sound as if he meant it. For Cruse, Trueheart was a symbol of all that was wrong with the System: selfish, autocratic, and sadistically cruel, it was said that the Security Chief's ambitions knew no bounds.

"Yes, it is a great honour, isn't it?" he said, and then pretended to notice the disks on the desk for the first time. He gingerly picked one up and examined it. "And what have we here then?"

Marla and Cruse exchanged anxious looks. "Some ... er, texts we were studying, Lord Trueheart," she said lamely.

"Really?" asked Trueheart. "How selfish of you," he continued. "Such things should be shared with everyone."

His voice suddenly took on a much more threatening tone. "And they should not be studied in a secret room which has been debugged, and which is designed to be beyond the range of even my finest security cameras and microphones!"

"I don't know what you're talking about!" said Marla.

"Donovan Trueheart sees all and knows all!" Trueheart declared. "I know what you were discussing in this room!"

"But how could ..." Cruse began, and then stopped as he realized just who had given them away to Donovan Trueheart.

Cruse had made sure that the room had been debugged but there was one thing he had forgotten about: the ServoRobot that was supposedly standing guard by the entrance to the room. He cursed himself. From that moment on Cruse knew that he would never trust another robot for as long as he might live.

Everyone had become so used to robots, so dependent on them, that they all forgot that, first and foremost, they were the servants of the System. They might be happy to make your tea, one of Cruse's more irreverent lecturers had once joked, but that was only so that they could tell the System just how many sugars you took.

"You have been questioning the righteousness of our great and glorious System," said Trueheart, in a voice which suggested that he took it as a personal insult.

"My Lord, we didn't mean to ..." began Corin, until Cruse shut him up with a look.

"That saddens me, truly it does," Trueheart continued. "The System is there for your benefit, my children, don't you realize that? Our civilization needs order. It needs efficiency, and trust, and faith. Without that we cannot live with each other; without that Mankind cannot achieve its – our – true potential."

"I'm sorry, Lord Trueheart," Marla said. "In future we'll..."

"Future?" repeated Trueheart, and shook his head.

"Oh, there will be no future for you." He turned to his guards who had now entered the room.

"Kill them," he said simply.

The jack-booted guards opened fire on the six students, sweeping the room in a hail of bullets. Cruse was the first to thud to the floor, screaming out in agony as the first bullets hit him. One caught Marla straight between the eyes, and she died instantly, not even having the time to cry out. As her lifeless body fell to the ground, even more bullets slammed mercilessly into her corpse.

Bullets thudded into Anya's frail figure and she fell jerkily to the floor, performing one last macabre dance of death for her assassins. Another projectile caught Corin in his chest and he was thrown back, splashing the floor with a stomach-turning mess of red.

When the final student had fallen, and the room was full of the bitter and rank smell of violent death, Donovan Trueheart ordered the guards to stop firing. He looked sadly at the carnage he had ordered and tut-tutted ironically.

"Let that be a lesson to you, my dears," he said, in a voice which suggested he was addressing a bunch of unruly schoolchildren rather than a blood-bespattered heap of corpses. "The System is here for everyone's benefit ... Don't abuse it by asking too many questions."

He swept out of the room, followed by the guards

and the ServoRobot which had betrayed Cruse and the others.

A deadly silence descended upon the room and several long minutes passed. And then someone moved, first cautiously, and then, when he was sure that all the guards had gone, Cruse shakily got to his feet.

He doubled up in pain: he had been wounded in the side. He knew it wasn't particularly serious and, with the proper medical attention, the injury would leave little more than an unpleasant scar.

He looked around at Marla and the others. They were all dead, of that there was no doubt. There was no way that they could have survived the onslaught of Trueheart's guards.

Cruse himself had only lived by quick thinking. An imperceptible half-instant before Trueheart's guards had opened fire, he had fallen to the floor, and played dead. Most of the guards' bullets had flown over him, and he had only sustained the relatively minor wound in his side. The others hadn't been so lucky, or sharp-witted; but then they – even Marla – still found it hard to believe that the System could be so vicious and so ruthless. Cruse, on the other hand, had always been criticized by his teachers at the Academy for having a questioning and suspicious nature; they said that it was a trait which he would do well to erase from his character, without suspecting that it would finally save his life.

Or guarantee my death, he suddenly realized, as he looked at the carcasses of his comrades. Cruse knew how the System worked, knew that it was encumbered by bureaucracy and staffed, at the lowest levels, by inefficient and frightened civil ser vants. When they came to collect the bodies, and if they bothered to count them, none of them would dare to announce to their superiors that one corpse had gone missing.

Cruse was officially dead, and, in spite of the circumstances, in spite of the stink of death which was rapidly filling the room, he knew exactly what that meant.

He was free, free of the System which claimed it cared for all its citizens, and mercilessly shot down all those who dared to disagree.

He was free of the machinations of power-hungry politicians like Donovan Trueheart who preached love and understanding and the dignity of the human being, and who was in a position of power precisely because the President wanted him close to her, where she could at least keep a watchful eye on him.

He was free of ServoRobots who were supposed to make life easier for mankind, but who, beneath their unmoving and unfeeling metal faces, were ready to betray their human masters at the first opportunity.

Cruse tore himself away from Marla's body and those of their friends. His eyes were full of tears, and he angrily brushed them away. He vowed that he would never cry again, never trust the System, never let another human being get close to him as Marla and the others had done. What was the point of loving someone, he asked himself, if they were to be taken away from you?

Without looking behind him, Cruse ran out of the room, a changed man. He knew where he had to go now, and the information he had taken from the Academy had told him what he had to do.

A strange sense of power and elation coursed through his entire body, as Cruse realized that he was no longer a part of the System. For the first time in seventeen years Cruse was a free man.

PART 1

Pasiphae

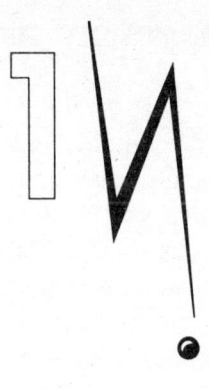

The Moons of Jupiter

Shari Sharifi gazed through her vid-glasses and up at the majestic towering splendour of St Paul's Cathedral and gasped. The magnificent Christopher Wren architecture, with its splendid spires and towers, simply took her breath away. Wren had been a mathematician and astronomer, as well as his country's leading architect, she recalled being taught, and it showed in his precise mathematical designs for the cathedral and the almost overpowering sense of space in the grand dome way above her head.

All that emptiness, serving no purpose at all, filled with nothing but the whispers of the past and the memories of the long-dead, she thought. There's room for at least two hundred living-units in that enormous dome alone. It's a totally irresponsible and unnecessary waste of space. And it's also quite wonderful!

Shari shook her head sadly, and ran her fingers through her long raven hair. On her home world of Pasiphae, one of the outermost moons of the great planet Jupiter, space was at a premium. After all, when a planet was as small as Pasiphae, and had to support at least one million people, you couldn't afford to misuse a single centimetre of space. Each citizen was given enough space in which to eat, sleep and live, and no more.

There was no room on Pasiphae for huge cathedrals, or wide open parks and recreational areas. The only open space on the planetoid was to be found in the Wastelands, and even there the landscape was cluttered up with the decaying remnants of the machines the humans had used in the past to terraform the moon of Jupiter. If it couldn't fit into a space four metres by four metres, Shari realized, then the Pasiphaean government wasn't interested in it. Certainly, words such as splendour, magnificence or grandeur were unknown to them.

Shari was used to these cramped living conditions by now, but there were still times when she longed for the wide-open spaces she'd seen on vid-disks, or read about in the few antique texts in her university library. She could only envy the travels taken by people her own age centuries ago, when they would take time off from their studies and hitch around the whole Earth, travelling from continent to continent, sailing on sea after sea. There was no sea on Pasiphae, and, as most Pasiphaeans would never be allowed off-world, most of them would live and die without ever having seen an ocean.

Shari longed to see an ocean, to taste the salt-tang of the sea-breeze on her lips, and the cries of the seagulls above the crashing of the waves. Until now it had been something that she'd only read about in books, or heard people who had travelled off-world speak about wistfully.

As a member of the ruling class of Pasiphae she knew that there was still the chance that she would be allowed to leave Pasiphae on an exchange trip to one of the neighbouring satellites, probably Amalthea, and she could hardly wait for her first trip out into the infinity of interplanetary space. There might not be oceans on Amalthea either, she realized, but deep space was reportedly the next best thing.

She looked up reverently at the interior of the cathedral again, running her gloved hands down the long cool stone pillars, and tracing the inscriptions on the walls with her long fingers.

There was no doubt about it: St Paul's was one of the most awe-inspiring monuments in the entire System, almost as impressive as India's Taj Mahal which she had visited this morning, or Egypt's Great Pyramid of Cheops which she had explored the previous day.

And like those other two monuments, St Paul's was no more, razed to the ground almost nine hundred years before Shari was born to make way for a new interplanetary spaceport.

Well, that's the System for you, she thought bitterly. If interplanetary government doesn't make a profit, who cares what it looks like: knock it down and build something that will.

Shari reached a hand up to the specially designed glasses, and adjusted a touch-sensitive control. Instantly the virtually-realized vision of St Paul's Cathedral in the Old London of 2377 snapped out of existence, and she was thudded cruelly back into reality.

She was sitting in one of the VR units – the Virtual Reality booths which were one of the most popular features of the Academy on Pasiphae. Here students could interface into any number of Virtual Reality programs, enabling them to travel from the long-devastated streets of New York in the late 21st century, to the sunny tree-lined streets of present-day New Canberra, and all at the flick of a switch.

It was just as good as the real thing, its proponents said, and as neither Shari nor any of her fellow students had ever experienced the "real thing" she would have to take them at their word. The only trouble with the program was that one could only go back in time as far as the middle years of the 21st century when, after a hundred years of experimentation, Virtual Reality technology was finally perfected.

She would have loved to have explored the temples of Old Bangkok, but they were destroyed before the golden age of Virtual Reality, along with most of the South-East Asian continent, and a fair chunk of the Indian sub-continent. She would have loved to have seen a forest too, but the Virtual Realizers who had set up their programmes had concentrated on the achievements of Mankind, rather than recording the wonders of Mother Nature.

Shari took off her glasses and tossed them onto the small table by the couch she was lying on. Then she removed the VR glove which had allowed her to "feel" the stones of the cathedral.

She felt a tingling in her fingers: that was common after a lengthy exploration of the disks in the VR library. And as a student with a special interest in Ancient Earth history Shari was more used than most to "visiting" archaeologically important sites on the old mother world.

As usual it took a few seconds for her eyes to adjust to "reality". She blinked and slowly the form of a young man, a little older than her, came into view. He gave a dazzling smile, showing her his flawlessly white teeth, and reached a hand over to help her off the couch. She was grateful for his assistance: a lengthy VR session often left her feeling drained and weak.

"Good trip?" the young man asked as Shari stumbled to her feet.

"One of the best, Kristas," she confirmed, before shrugging her shoulders helplessly. "And one of the last . . ." she added sadly.

"Look on the bright side, Shari," he said.

Shari chuckled ironically. "You do enough of that for the both of us," she pointed out not unkindly. "If we were in the path of a giant comet which would wipe out all life here you'd still want to go outside and watch the firework display."

"I just like to see the best in everything, that's all," Kristas laughed. "And everyone."

"Well, you tell me what reason I've got to be so cheerful then?"

"You've just graduated from the Academy with straight As," he reminded her. "You should be proud of yourself: you're the first student to do that in years."

"I know and that's what's worrying me," she admitted, and then was suddenly serious. "Kristas, for the past few years at the Academy I've had a wonderful time studying. . ."

Kristas pooh-poohed the idea. "Ancient Earth history? That's all in the past, as dead as those dinosaurs you're so fond of," he said disparagingly. "Where's the fun in that?"

Shari shook her head. She was a scientist first and foremost and Kristas was ... well, Kristas was a dreamer. That was probably why they got on so well together: they complemented each other perfectly.

"I've been allowed unlimited access to the VR libraries," she reminded him. "Over the past two years I've 'visited' each and every one of the twenty-one Wonders of the System. I've even seen the Martian canals by moonlight, and watched dawn break over the Pompidou Centre in Paris—"

"Where?" Kristas asked.

"Paris," she explained. "It was the capital of a country they called France."

"Another ruin then," said Kristas, but there was a sympathetic glint in his ice-blue eyes: he had an idea what was worrying Shari: he'd experienced the same sort of unrequited wanderlust from time to time himself.

"And now I'll have to give all that up," she said. "Give up the only freedom I'm allowed to have."

"We all of us have to, y'know," he said. "I had to when I graduated last year. We have to grow up sometime and become responsible citizens, and work within the System."

"You're a linguist, Kristas, your skills are required all over Pasiphae," she pointed out.

The Jovian satellite had been colonized for over a quarter of a century now but still its new inhabitants, drawn from all the diverse races of the planet that had once been called the Earth, couldn't decide on a common tongue. "Your interpreting work takes you from pole to pole."

"What's the big deal?" he asked flippantly. "I speak ten Old Earth languages, plus several patois, and four different signings. And all I do is translate the grumbles and demands of whining administrators."

Shari looked around, almost instinctively: one never knew when one was being listened to on Pasiphae. "But at least you get to travel," she insisted and lowered her voice. "That's rare enough these days."

Travelling was officially frowned upon on Pasiphae. Indeed, it was quite common for a person to be born, spend the whole of their life and die in the same small conurbation.

Lately, however, travel restrictions had become even more stringent, although no one quite knew why. There had been talk about mysterious space plagues but as usual the Board, the local government, was saying as little as possible.

Kristas shrugged the idea off. "Once you've seen one mercury swamp, Shari, you've seen them all."

"That's not it and you know it," she said grudgingly, trying hard to conceal her anger.

Doesn't he realize just how lucky he is? she asked herself. Virtual Reality is all very well, but it doesn't beat getting out there and experiencing the real thing!

"So I once gained a special dispensation to travel off-world," Kristas continued nonchalantly, even though he felt rather awkward at the direction the conversation was taking.

His eyes glanced around the room too, but no one seemed to be paying any attention to them. "There was a border dispute on Amalthea," he said, referring to one of the neighbouring moons of Jupiter. "They needed someone with knowledge of Twenty-Ninth Century Slavic. It was no big deal, Shari," he lied.

Shari wasn't taken in for a minute. She had known Kristas since they had been children, and, ever since her father had mysteriously disappeared when she was nine, she had always regarded him as her best friend, and the big brother she had never had.

She remembered long walks they had taken on the rocky plains outside Galileo, the main settlement of the newly terraformed planet. Such excursions weren't exactly forbidden by the System, but were regarded as a harmless caprice. After all, the System had once said, our citizens are free to go wherever they want on-world; why make an area off-limits to the few eccentrics who would like to go there?

They breathed through respirators: even though the Terraformers had provided Pasiphae with a breathable atmosphere of sorts, the air outside the main domed settlements and towns was still weak in oxygen content and high in methane. The respirators compensated for the weakness of the atmosphere, even if Kristas had complained more than once that they were clumsy, ugly and unwieldy; not that it mattered: most Pasiphaeans never left the warm and secure domes of their home settlements.

The sky, as always, was dominated by the dirty-yellow hazy sphere of Jupiter, the largest planet in the entire Solar System. Its famous red spot gazed down on Shari and Kristas, like the malevolent red eye of a scornful god, expressing his contempt for the tiny race of humans who, like lice, had dared to colonize his children, after they had ruined their own Home Planet.

Shari had always been impressed, even awed, by the enormous size of the planet: it made her both aware of her own insignificance in the face of it, and it strangely inspired her.

She knew that a few industrial air-bases had been set up in Jupiter's atmosphere, skimming the planet's gaseous surface like boats on an ocean, and mining its valuable minerals and gases. Most Pasiphaeans, however, had never been allowed to leave their adopted world and journey, even briefly, to any of the other Jovian satellites, let alone Jupiter itself.

Even fewer had been granted permission to travel outside Jupiter's orbit, to the moons of that other great gas giant, Saturn; and it was unheard of that anyone had ever gone to TerraNova, the new administrative centre of the entire System government which, in a time long gone (so Shari's vid-disks had told her) had once been known as the planet Mars.

As Shari and Kristas had stared up into the night

sky, past the haze of light coming from Jupiter, and into the purple-blackness of space, studded with the lights of distant stars twinkling like so many specks of platinum dust, she had noticed the yearning in her old friend's eyes.

He too longed to travel amongst those platinum-specks, wanted the freedom to travel off-world whenever he wanted, and not just when System decreed that he should settle some local dispute on Amalthea.

Tired of life on Pasiphae, which was as grey and dull as the clinker and waste which surrounded the main town of Galileo, he longed for new and exciting experiences. Shari, too, had many reasons for wanting to go off-world, of which her love of Earth history was only one.

"It was no big deal," he had told her.

Who's he trying to kid! I've seen that gleam in his eyes when he looks at the stars. He wants to get off Pasiphae as much as I do!

"Maybe not to you ..." she said grudgingly.

Kristas put a brotherly arm around her. "What's wrong with you?" he asked. "You've been edgy all week."

Shari shrugged him off. "It's Graduation Day today," she explained. "The day I get to find out what my future will be..."

"Ah..."

Graduation Day was the most significant and

traumatic day in the life of any young person of the Pasiphaean ruling class. It was the day when the Board, those faceless bureaucrats and administrators responsible for the smooth-running of all aspects of life on Pasiphae, decided the future.

On this day each Academician was allotted his or her task in life. The Board decided where a graduate was to live, and with the aid of the latest bio-computer technology even which career they were best suited for. There could be no appeal, no redress, no going-back on whatever decision was arrived at: what the Board decided became instant and irrevocable law.

Kristas had been lucky, Shari realized, and had been given a life-task which at least suited his personality; but she had no idea what the Board had in store for her. She had heard stories about graduates being wrenched from their families and cut off from all their friends, when they were given a life-time posting to the poles. There had even been talk of suicide amongst those for whom the Board's decision had been cruelly inappropriate, and Shari knew of at least one fellow student who had mysteriously vanished before Graduation Day. They said that he had run off into Shantyland, there to join other misfits and rejects from society. If it was true, Shari couldn't help but have a sneaking admiration for him.

What did the Board have in store for her?

"I'm to report to the Board in three hours' time,"

she said and looked searchingly at Kristas. "Be there with me."

Kristas looked awkwardly away, avoiding her eyes. He took a deep breath: "I'm sorry, Shari, I can't..."

Shari frowned. "You're my best friend, Kristas," she said, genuinely puzzled by his refusal. "You're the closest I have to family. I *need* you there!"

"I'm sorry, Shari..."

His voice trailed off: he knew he was letting her down badly. "I just can't..."

"What d'you mean, you just can't?" she snapped, her quick temper suddenly getting the better of her. "This is the most important day of my life, and you can't even be bothered to turn up for it?" By now Shari's voice was raised, and several fellow students were looking at them curiously.

"Shari, don't start an argument here," he said, taking hold of her arm. She shrugged him off, but moved into a corner, away from the stares of the others.

"What have you got to do that's so important then?" she demanded sarcastically. "Another day trip to Amalthea maybe? Or perhaps you're going for the big time now – a jaunt down to Jupiter to sort out some industrial dispute?"

"Shari, I can't tell you," he said lamely, still avoiding her eyes. "It's too important for me..."

"So important that you'll walk off and leave me alone to face those mindless bureaucrats?" she sneered. "I was there last year when you graduated, wasn't I? I thought we were friends."

Kristas looked up into Shari's eyes: they were misty with the tears she refused to let fall.

"We are friends, Shari ..." he insisted.

"Well, you've sure a great way of showing it," she retorted, and then her voice softened.

"Please, Kristas," she said. "You know the decisions of the Board are final. If they send me off to some research institute in another conurbation we might never see each other again..."

Kristas hesitated. Shari was his closest friend: he owed it to her to offer support at this stressful time.

Well, I owe something to myself as well, he reasoned with himself. This is my one and only chance, and I can't pass it by.

"I'm sorry, Shari," he said with genuine regret. "I can't explain now. But believe me, you'd do the same as me ... if only you knew..."

Shari looked strangely at her old friend, and realized that he was going through as much pain and hurt as she was. They had always trusted each other and had never before had any secrets from each other: what was he trying to hide from her now? Whatever it was, it was obviously so important to him that he was prepared to put their friendship on the line.

But there's nothing that could be that important to Kristas, she thought.

Or is there?

"What is it, Kristas?" she asked. "What won't you tell me?"

Kristas bit his lip. He needed to tell someone. Ever since the Board had approached him two months ago, he had longed to unburden himself, to share the news he had been given with another person.

Shari could be trusted, he reasoned; surely his secret would be safe with her? He looked around to make sure that no one else was listening and took a deep breath.

"It's the ... the Seti ..." he whispered.

Shari frowned, and looked blankly at him. "The Seti?"

Kristas hushed her. "Not so loud, not here!"

"I don't understand, Kristas," she said, more quietly this time. "What's the Seti?"

"Not what, *who*," he said, and was about to say more when they were approached by one of Shari's fellow students.

A short, weaselly-looking boy, Jared had a reputation for being the class creep, making up for what he lacked in brains by gaining his teachers' favours with oily obsequiousness. Kristas had always made allowances for him; Shari, with more characteristic candour, simply said that he made her itch every time she looked at him. He eyed up Shari and Kristas suspiciously.

"And what are you two lovebirds up to then?" he oozed.

"We're not lovebirds," retorted Shari. "And we were just having a conversation – one that doesn't include you."

Jared shrugged, and shambled off towards the Virtual Reality booths. Shari glared after him.

"Loathsome toad," she said with uncharitable venom. She was suddenly aware that by her side Kristas was shaking: his face was as white as a sheet.

"Kristas, what is it?" she asked. "What's up?"

Kristas continued to watch Jared as he sat down and plugged himself into the VR equipment. Jared's parents were influential administrators on Pasiphae. How much had he heard and understood? How much might he tell them?

"There's nothing the matter, Shari," he lied, and made for the door. He glanced once more at Jared and then turned to Shari. "Look, I'm sorry I can't make your Graduation," he said guiltily, "but ... good luck anyway."

"But Kristas, what about—"

But Kristas was gone before she had even finished her sentence. Shari watched his departing figure knowingly. He hadn't fooled her one bit. Something was worrying Kristas, and indeed had been for the past few months, of that she was certain. And whatever it was it had something to do with the Seti – whoever he or she might be.

And then Shari frowned, as a long-forgotten memory struggled to call out to her from the back of her mind. Perhaps she had heard that strange name somewhere else before after all. A long, long time ago...

"Seti, Seti..."

She repeated the name silently to herself, and an inexplicable shiver of delight and anticipation ran down her spine. In her mind she could hear the word being repeated over and over again – not in her own voice, but in the voice of the person she had first heard using that word.

The voice in her head was that of her father, Jarrl, the father she had not seen for nine long years. Somehow Jarrl and the Seti were connected.

Graduation Day

Shari flung herself down on her bed in her small room in the hostel which she shared with her fellow students at the Academy during term-time. It was the one place, apart from a VR booth, where she was allowed a bit of welcome privacy.

A normal day was usually spent studying in the company of her fellow students, or taking part in activities which would better prepare them for their roles as future administrators of Pasiphae.

No one on Pasiphae was allowed a life of leisure or inactivity; each and every citizen was expected to partake fully in the smooth running of the satellite. Because of its proximity to Jupiter, most of Pasiphaean life was connected in one way or another to the exploitation of Jupiter's precious gases and minerals; from her studies of early Earth history Shari had long ago recognized the similarities between Pasiphae and the old mining towns on Earth. The existence of valuable minerals on one's back doorstep ensured the continued prosperity of Pasiphae even though few of those minerals were used to improve the lot of the native population. Most of what was mined on Jupiter and the outer satellites was reportedly shipped immediately back to TerraNova.

Although what use they have for all this stuff is beyond me, she thought to herself.

She often wondered what would happen to life on Pasiphae when mighty Jupiter's resources were finally exhausted in a few centuries' time. By then Pasiphae would have outlived its usefulness to the scientists back on TerraNova: what would become of the Pasiphaeans then? Perhaps they would be moved back to TerraNova, which had been colonized in the late 22nd century and completely terraformed only a hundred years later in one of the greatest engineering feats in mankind's history.

Some people have all the luck, she thought glumly, realizing that her chances of leaving Pasiphae and exploring the supposed wonders of Mankind's new home world were practically nil, except in Virtual Reality.

She looked at the chronometer which hung on the wall at the foot of her bed. There were still two hours to go before she was due to have her future decided once and for all by the Board. For a moment she idly toyed with the idea of asking one of her fellow students to accompany her there; but there was no one she really trusted, except Kristas.

Of course, it would have been different if her father, Jarrl, had been around; but she hadn't seen him for almost nine years now. They said that he'd died, killed in a space shuttle accident on a rare trip down to the surface of Jupiter. But she had depended on her father for so much that she couldn't bring herself to believe that; to imagine herself alone in the world was unbearable. And when she'd asked Kili, who had brought her up since then, he'd just chuckled meaningfully to himself and been evasive as only he could be.

She activated the holo-album, and a hologram of Jarrl shot up into life on the screen. A tall, thick-set and handsome physicist with Shari's own jet-black hair; it was how she remembered him. He must have been in his early forties when he left her mysteriously one night.

She closed her eyes and willed back the last time she had seen him alive. He'd been acting strangely for a long time, and occasionally had even snapped angrily at her, something he had never done since the death of her mother two years previously. He'd also been away from their apartment for longer and longer periods, entrusting her welfare to the much-loved and ever-reliable Kili.

That night Shari had been sent to bed earlier than usual and had found it difficult to sleep. She'd tried to amuse herself by looking through her collection of old fossils which her father had brought back from TerraNova, and, when even that had failed to erase the worries nagging at the back of her mind, she had sneaked downstairs to her father's study and peeked through the half-open door.

Her father had a visitor. That in itself was nothing unusual – as a top-ranking scientist he often conducted meetings in his study long into the night with fellow scientists. And yet there was something different about this visitor, something different in the way her father treated him. With his work-colleagues Jarrl had a jovial, back-slapping, all-scientists-together manner; but now Jarrl's broad shoulders were hunched and there was a strange tone of respect in his voice.

Shari peered through the gloom of the darkened study to see who the stranger was. To the seven-year-old Shari he seemed unimaginably old, and in the half-light of the study she could see his parchment-brown skin stretched tautly over his sharp cheekbones. He was aged and wrinkled, and yet he carried himself with an air of power and authority; his eyes, which should have been blurred and rheumy, sparkled with a fierce intelligence. He was tall and thin, with a shock of white hair, and was standing, leaning on a walking stick.

Shari struggled to hear what her father and his visitor were saying, but they were speaking in hushed whispers. She could catch only the odd word, and understood none of those.

What was apparent though was that her father was very worried and very angry indeed. From time to time he would leap up out of his chair and shout at the old man, who just remained standing there, showing no emotion whatsoever.

"I cannot do it!" she heard her father saying. "I have my work here!"

"We need you, Jarrl." Shari could hardly hear the old man, his voice was so cracked and soft. "Your skill is invaluable to us. You are an extremely skilled and talented physicist."

That pleased the eavesdropping Shari: she'd always known that her daddy was a genius.

"You cannot force me to do anything," Jarrl continued. "If I choose to say no you cannot make me agree to your request..."

"Of course not," came the old man's reply, but it somehow seemed, even to the young Shari, insincere. "The System is a society of equals. No one individual is better than any other individual..."

Well, I'm certainly better than that drippy Jared! Shari thought angrily, as she recalled getting into a fight with the son of one of her father's friends. At least I don't smell!

"And as a society of equals, we cannot force

anyone to do anything against their own will." The old man's voice was deeply ironic now. "We can however, help our citizens to choose the path that might be right for them."

Shari watched as the old man hobbled over to the holo-image in the corner of the room. It was a hologram of Shari and Jarrl. Shari smiled: she knew that Jarrl always liked to brag about her and tell everybody just how well she was doing in her studies. But when Jarrl saw the old man looking at the holo-image his face fell.

The old man turned back from the holo-image and regarded Jarrl with saturnine and manipulative eyes. "I see you have a daughter, Jarrl, a very pretty young daughter indeed..."

"Leave Shari out of this!" Jarrl snapped.

The old man sighed theatrically. "Unfortunately I cannot leave Shari out of this," he said.

"What d'you mean?" asked Jarrl. "If you so much as harm one hair on my daughter's head..."

"Then let us hope that it won't come to that," he said, and now there was ice in the old man's voice. "Let us hope that you will agree to our proposal."

Shari was considering whether she should try and sneak into the study where she could hear more when she felt a long, bony, metallic hand on her shoulder.

Uh-oh, caught snooping again! she thought and looked up guiltily.

Kili was staring down at her disapprovingly as only a Mark Seven ServoRobot could. The red visor-like slit which served as his visual circuits blinked open and shut, and from out of the circular grille, which Shari liked to think of as his mouth, there came a series of irritated clicks.

"And shouldn't you be in bed by now, young lady?" Kili asked. His voice was tinny, and full of self-importance.

Shari's face fell as the seven-foot Kili bent down and lifted her up into his arms. They were bony but enormously powerful; made of parondite, one of the toughest alloys ever invented, they could smash their way through six-feet concrete as easily as Shari might rip a sheet of paper.

"Aw, Kili, I wanted to see who Daddy was talking to," Shari said as she snuggled against Kili's breastplate, the temperature of which Kili automatically increased to human body temperature for her comfort.

"Your father is talking to a very important official from the System," Kili revealed, as he carried her back to her bedroom, "and it's important that he isn't disturbed."

"But why shouldn't he be disturbed?" she asked petulantly.

Kili gave the robotic equivalent of a sigh. "Don't ask questions, Shari," he reproved.

"But I like asking questions!" she countered, and yawned.

"And all these questions are making you tired," Kili said, as they entered Shari's bedroom. Shari frowned as he laid her on the bed. The robot's normally monotone voice now sounded as if he was unhappy. And that's impossible 'cos robots don't have feelings, she reminded herself.

"Kili, is there anything wrong?" she asked, her curiosity about her father's visitor suddenly forgotten.

"Of course not," Kili clicked irritably as he adjusted her covers. "Now go to sleep."

"OK," she said. "But not before you tell me a story..."

"I'm a Mark Seven ServoRobot capable of deeds beyond the imagination of common man – I can survive temperatures approaching absolute zero, can live quite comfortably in the methane swamps of Jupiter, and can smash through six-feet concrete with my bare hands – and you want me to tell you a story?"

"Yup," said Shari and giggled under the sheets.

Kili sighed again. What use were all his powers in the face of his young charge's persuasive ways? He knew when he was beaten.

"Very well," he said. "And what story should I tell you?"

Shari considered for a second. "My favourite," she said. "You know, the one about long ago on the

Home Planet, when it was still called the Earth . . . the one about the dinosaurs. . .''

That was the last time she had seen her father alive, although that night she dreamed that he had come into her bedroom and kissed her on the forehead. His face was lined and drawn and there were tears in his eyes.

The following morning Kili told her that Jarrl had been called away to an important conference at one of the mines on the surface of Jupiter. A few days later the robot broke the news to her that he had been killed in a space shuttle accident. Even since then Kili had brought her up.

Shari's world was devastated. First her mother had died and now her father. Yet she had little time to grieve. The following year she had been granted a place at the Academy, the prestigious school on Pasiphae, reserved for the children of top-ranking members of System government or the Board, and her life was soon taken over completely by her studies.

What was more, at eight years old, she was a year younger than the other first-year students at the Academy. Most people said that she had got into the Academy on her own merits, which were indeed impressive. However, many of the older students – including the odious Jared – wondered what strings had been pulled on her behalf. However, as Shari pointed out, she had no one who could pull strings for her; with both her parents dead there was only Kili, and who would listen to a robot, even one as opinionated and persuasive as Kili?

And yet. . . .

Even as her grief over her father's death passed she could never quite bring herself to believe that he was truly dead. The space shuttle had disintegrated on contact with Jupiter's surface and no trace of wreckage or bodies had ever been found, or, indeed, looked for. Kristas, who was in the year above her, had told her that that was by no means unusual. He had lost both his parents in a similar accident, and he understood what she was going through. As time went on they discovered that they had more in common than just their being orphans and they soon became firm friends.

"I was like you," Shari, he had told her. "You try and deny to yourself the fact that you will never see someone you loved so much again. But in time you get over it. Time really does heal everything, Shari . . ." At which Shari had shrugged and tried to put a brave face on it, saying that Kristas was very probably right.

And yet. . . .

There were times when Shari was studying late into the night when she thought someone was watching her. She'd turn to the vid-phone by her bed, and see the little red control light quickly blink off, as if someone was trying to contact her and had thought better of it at the very last moment.

Then there were the tiny gifts Kili would sometimes give her: small ammonites, and rocks, whose provenance he refused to disclose. Such things could only have come from the Home Planet, or one of the museums on TerraNova. Since all robots were forbidden to travel off-world how could he have come by them?

Nor would Kili say where the credits to finance her studies really came from. He had claimed that the System government had acknowledged responsibility for the accident in which Jarrl had died, and had provided a stipend to support Shari until her studies were completed and she could become a useful member of Pasiphaean society. Somehow that didn't ring true: the System being so generous was highly unlikely.

As Shari grew older her father's supposed death seemed to her to become more and more suspicious, although she never asked questions publicly. Even his behaviour before his disappearance seemed odd. He had been tetchy and secretive about his affairs, when normally he had been so open about everything. Indeed, along with Kristas her father was the most easy-going and trusting person she knew.

And now Kristas was being tetchy and secretive too, she realized sadly, and switched off the holo-album. The image of her father vanished from the screen.

There was a tap at the door of her room and the

door swished open. Kili was standing outside holding in his arms a baby chimpanzee. When the chimp saw Shari it leapt out of the robot's arms and scampered over to Shari, who picked her up.

"I thought you might need some company today," said Kili as he bent down to pass through the doorway, "especially as Kristas isn't here."

"Thanks, Kili," she said, as she cuddled her pet chimp, Doob. Then she frowned. "How did you know that Kristas isn't around?" she asked.

Kili paused and Shari could almost hear the wheels of his computerized mind going round. He made a clicking sound, which Shari had learnt to recognize as his equivalent of blushing red with embarrassment, and finally said: "I, er, met him on the way here ... Are you ready?"

"For being told what those stuffed old shirts, the Board, have got in store for me?" she said gloomily and shrugged. "As ready as I'll ever be, I suppose..."

"It's a great honour to graduate from the Academy with top grades," Kili pointed out to her. "It's only the very few who get chosen to contribute to our planet's welfare. You have a great future ahead of you, Shari."

"Yeah, I know," she replied, clearly not enthralled by the prospect at all. "With any luck I might even get a return ticket to one of the mines of Jupiter. And won't that be exciting then?" she added sarcastically.

"You're far too flippant, Shari," he reproved, as he led her out of the door. He paused and turned to her.

"I have looked after your welfare ever since your father died, Shari; and I am very proud of you."

Shari was genuinely touched. She grinned awkwardly and joked: "You can't be proud, Kili. You're a robot; two and a half tons of parondite alloy and microcircuits. You're not supposed to have any emotions."

"Ah of course," he replied. "I had forgotten that ... Now come along, Shari, you can't be late for the most important day of your life!"

One Year to Earth

The egg-shaped craft slowed down once again as it approached the dead planet Pluto, and its twin-world Charon. It had entered planetary space now, and would have to sail with more caution if it was to avoid the space detritus, and the artificial satellites and beacons with which Mankind had littered its own solar system over the past thousand years. One chance collision with a still active satellite could result in an explosion so colossal that the ship and its crew would be instantly destroyed. Death meant very little to the pilots of this ship, but the success of their mission was paramount.

Within the starship strange three-fingered claws activated this lever and that navigational display, constantly adjusting and fine-tuning each and every control on board.

A stream of static flowed out of the audio-circuits built into the control consoles which seemed to line every wall in the mighty machine, scanning the solar system for those regular patterns of radiation which would indicate the presence of intelligent life. The radio waves emitted in their billions every day from TerraNova and its colony worlds were better than any homing beacon for guiding the ship in safety to its destination.

A hiss of delight came from the Chief Navigator as he fixed and cross-referenced one particular energy source. He rasped the news on to his companions and, as he did so, huge globs of thick acidic saliva dripped from his mouth and fell onto the control panel before him.

No one noticed: every single blood-shot and lid-less eye was concentrated on their revised flight path which was now displayed on the huge navigation screen.

An ugly chittering sound arose from the assembled crowd, as they celebrated the approaching end of their journey. By their side, daring to venture out from the gloomy shadows of the far part of the navigation room, two small and hunched hairy creatures also came to take a look. They each shuffled forwards on two legs to take a furtive look at the image on the screen.

They frowned, and in their tiny dark eyes there was a sudden but brief flash of understanding. The coloured patterns on the screen were pretty and pleased them; they looked at each other and grinned, grunting their pleasure to each other.

The Chief Navigator suddenly registered their presence and shooed them away, as a man would a particularly troublesome dog. The two hairy creatures scrambled back into the shadows, and cowered.

In the dank green gloom of the spacecraft they could easily have been mistaken for two very old and shrunken human beings. Their masters, on the other hand, were anything but human...

Academician Shari Sharifi

Shari looked up at the yellow globe of Jupiter and cried. In her arms she cuddled Doob, who whimpered, aware of her mistress's distress but unsure how to console her. She had been standing outside on the balcony of her dormitory for the past hour now, just staring out into space.

Blast the Board! she cursed. Blast their narrow-minded, unimaginative bureaucracy! Blast Kristas! And blast the whole of Pasiphae!

Doob nuzzled her neck, and Shari smiled. "What's going to happen to us now, Doob?" she asked, and then laughed bitterly. "Or rather what's *not* going to happen to us now?"

Her interview with the Board had ended an hour ago and she had now officially graduated from the

Academy, a fully-fledged Academician and member of adult society.

"Your grades have been excellent, Ms Sharifi," the head of the Board had droned on in his grim and soulless voice. "You have shown an extremely hard-working and methodical approach, especially in your researches into the anthropology and architecture of Old Earth. We feel that these qualities ideally equip you for the life-career that has been selected for you. . ."

At those words Shari's heart had leapt in her breast. It could only mean that they were to send her to TerraNova itself, or even to the Home Planet. At last she could get off this boring little planetoid with its petty regulations and constrictions on personal liberty!

At last she would have the freedom to travel among the stars, to experience for the first time the wide-open spaces where the skyline was not dominated by row upon row of faceless work and housing units.

". . . And therefore, Ms Sharifi," the voice continued, "it has been decided that you shall be removed to Conurbation Two in the southern hemisphere of Pasiphae, where you will work on cataloguing and ordering the Board's archives. For the rest of your life. You may go now, Ms Sharifi."

It had sounded like an execution sentence and for Shari it might just as well have been. She was to be stuck on Pasiphae until she died – and that, she realized, would probably be of boredom. She was just sixteen years old. She couldn't face the prospect of spending the rest of her life buried deep within the minutiae of System life, working with a bunch of old crusty archivists and administrators.

Once again she realized the full implication of the perfect and smoothly-run life that the System had set up for her on Pasiphae. Life was relatively easy, they said, compared to some of the other planets in the System, and its proximity to Jupiter ensured that theirs was a prosperous world. Most of its admittedly stringent laws seemed to be fair and set up for the well-being of its citizens. You could hardly compare life on Pasiphae to the totalitarian dictatorships in the 20th century, Shari knew. No Pasiphaean lacked anything they might ever need, except one thing they were forever denied – freedom to travel.

She looked back up into the sky, and at the faraway stars which once had seemed so full of promise and now just seemed to be mocking her.

I cannot do what the Board has decided, she vowed to herself. I cannot spend the rest of my life knowing that I can never travel out there among the stars!

Doob started to chirp in her arms as she became aware of a newcomer. Shari turned around to see Kristas standing there. His normally well-groomed hair was mussed and untidy and his eyes were red and puffy. If Shari hadn't known him better she could have sworn that he had been crying.

"Kristas?" She put Doob down on the ground, who happily trotted over to Kristas, and brushed an unshed tear from her eye. She hated people to know that she had been crying. "How long have you been standing there?"

"Long enough." He smiled weakly and walked over to her side. Leaning on the balcony rail he joined her in looking out at the stars.

"They're beautiful, aren't they?" he said dreamily. "And to think that there's so much life out there..."

"What d'you mean?" Shari asked, catching a new tone in his voice.

"On Amalthea, and the moons of Saturn, and the asteroids, and TerraNova," he said quickly, referring to all the worlds of the Solar System that mankind had colonized in a thousand years of pioneering yet limited space travel.

"If you say so," Shari said grumpily. "I don't suppose I'll ever have the chance to find out now..."

Kristas laid a sympathetic hand on her shoulder. "I'm sorry," he said. "I should have been there..."

"It doesn't matter," she lied.

"Oh yes, it does," he said. "Who'd want to be an archivist for the rest of their lives in Conurbation Two? Filing documents, cross-referencing infobites in a dusty old library ... How long till you leave?"

"A week ..." Shari turned to him. "Wait a minute,

how do you know what the Board's decided for me? I've told no one about it yet ..." She smiled down at her pet chimp, who was busy scratching under her arm. "Well, apart from Doob, that is, and I don't think she'd tell on me."

"Kili told me," he said. "He also told me that you were up here."

Shari frowned. "Kili? But I haven't seen him since ... Wait a minute, how did he know?"

Kristas shrugged. "You know what Kili's like," he chuckled. "He's an incorrigible snoop!"

Clearly for Kristas there was nothing suspicious at all in the robot's knowledge; even Shari could remember times when her old friend had seemed to have known much more about her private life than he should have done.

"So what do you think you'll do now?" he asked.

"What else can I do?" she said through gritted teeth. "You know that the Board's decision is final. There's no escape. Not unless you go to Shanty-Land..."

"Somehow I can't see you running away into the Wastelands," he laughed. "Joining that bunch of Misfits and ne'er-do-wells."

Shari smiled. "Maybe not ..." She looked around, as if to check that no one was watching them from one of the neighbouring balconies, and then lowered her voice: "But sometimes I admire them – those people who've dropped out of society, and left the conurbations to make their own lives away from the rulings of the Board."

"They're also illegal," Kristas pointed out to her, echoing the cant which had been taught to everyone who had ever attended the Academy. "A threat to the stability of Pasiphae."

Shari grinned in spite of herself. Kristas was a dreamer, there was no doubt of that, but he never had the initiative to make his dreams reality. Shari, on the other hand, was the reverse: she had no time for dreaming – she liked to make things happen. She turned back to look up at the stars again.

"What did you mean when you said that there's so much life out there?" she asked.

Kristas flushed. "I told you – on Amalthea, the moons of Saturn—"

"I know what you told me," Shari interrupted him. "But what did you *mean*?"

Kristas didn't reply. There was an awkward silence before Shari asked: "Where were you today? What was so special that you couldn't come with me?"

Kristas continued to look up at the stars and didn't reply.

"No one can hear us out here, Kristas," she said, but still he wouldn't speak.

"What did you mean there's so much life out there?" she persisted, gently but firmly; and then, remembering their conversation yesterday, added: "Kristas, who is the Seti?"

"I'll never find out now . . ." he muttered, not quite under his breath.

"Tell me, Kristas," she urged.

Long seconds passed and then Kristas turned away from the stars, and looked at Shari. He had lived with the secret for long months now; he had to tell someone. And who cared if Shari was wrong and there was someone listening?

"You don't know," he said. "No one on Pasiphae knows. Or on any other of the moon colonies, for that matter. After all the trouble on TerraNova the System's decided it's better to keep it a secret. . ."

"What trouble, Kristas? Keep what secret?" she asked, irritably. "*Tell me!*"

Kristas took a long deep breath. "A long time ago, long before Earth was abandoned, there was something called the SETI project."

"Seti?"

"It stood for the Search for Extra-Terrestrial Intelligence," he continued. "We sent out radio waves into space, hoping that someone would pick up on them. . ."

The name suddenly seemed familiar again, and once again Shari could see her father's face in her mind's eye. Shari tried to recall a conversation Jarrl had had with her mother a long, long time ago. Hadn't they spoken of the Seti then? She told Kristas to continue.

"Well, someone did," Kristas revealed.

"You mean ..." The importance of what Kristas was telling her was almost too much for her to comprehend.

"We received a reply in 2169, over a thousand years ago," he whispered. "An alien race out there had picked up on our signals and returned our message."

"What did they say?"

"Who knows?" He shrugged. "It was just a repetitive pulse, indicating that they had identified our signal as coming from an intelligent civilization."

"It couldn't have been a quasar or a pulsar, could it?" she asked sensibly.

Kristas shook his head. "There were slight fluctuations in its rhythm," he said. "It had to be artificial. Over the next hundred years their signal started growing stronger and stronger."

"Stronger and stronger?"

"Whatever's transmitting those signals isn't planet-based, Shari." Kristas looked back up at the stars. "It's *moving*. They're coming to visit us!"

Shari suddenly found that she was shaking all over. "Another race – there are other intelligent people out there ..." she joined Kristas in glancing up at the starry sky, "and they're coming to the System?"

"That's right. The scientists on Earth called them the Seti, after the name of the project."

A strange new mix of elation and apprehension coursed through Shari's body.

"But ... but that's wonderful," she breathed.

The idea of an entirely new culture just waiting to be discovered, the realization that that great black empty void was no longer empty, and that Man wasn't alone in the Universe, filled her with tremendous joy and excitement.

And then she remembered the pulp adventure novels that some of her schoolfriends had greedily devoured: they were all full of alien monsters attacking and enslaving Mankind. There was something she'd read once called *The War of the Worlds* by a writer whose name she had forgotten. Aliens had come down to Earth and practically rendered the human race extinct.

"At least, I think it's wonderful..."

An eminently sensible idea struck her and she looked suspiciously at Kristas, suspecting that he was teasing her.

"Wait a minute, this is the biggest news of the century," she said. "Why haven't we heard anything about it?"

"They know about it on TerraNova, or at least there are rumours on the streets," Kristas revealed. "And they feel the same as you: should we welcome the aliens, or are they a threat to us? There have been riots in the streets..."

This was news to Shari, and she said so.

"There's an embargo on news," he said in answer to her unspoken question. "When was the last time anyone from Pasiphae travelled to TerraNova, or anyone from Mars travelled here?"

"The System has kept it secret," she realized. "Then how did you find out?"

"I'm a linguist, Shari."

"So?" Shari couldn't see how Kristas's skills made him privy to this world-shattering secret.

"When the Seti finally arrive in the System we'll have to communicate with them in some way," he said. "I understand the theory and structure of both spoken and visual language. The System's going to need skilled linguists to try and understand their language."

Shari's eyes opened wide. "And you're to go to TerraNova to meet them!" She hugged her friend. "Kristas, that's wonderful!"

Kristas pulled away from her embrace and shook his head sadly. "Not any more. They turned me down at the final selection committee."

Suddenly Shari realized why Kristas had been unable to attend her graduation. "That's why you couldn't come with me," she said, and Kristas nodded.

He angrily turned away and smashed his fist into the palm of his hand. "All the members of the System team wanted me to go," he said ruefully. "They said that I would be an ideal member of the interpreting team. All of them, that is, except that one white-haired man with the cane."

With a cane? A memory of the past shot, unwelcome, into Shari's mind and she hugged Doob even tighter. Hadn't that man who had come to visit her father also carried a cane? Surely it was just a coincidence.

And yet...

"So what will you do now?" she asked him gently.

Kristas laughed bitterly. "Stay on Pasiphae," he said. "They'll never let me off-world now. I'm a security risk now. They'll probably transfer me to some isolated outpost where I'll spend the rest of my days translating old texts into even older Anglo-Saxon. I'm sworn to secrecy, you see."

"Then why are you telling me?" Shari asked.

Kristas laughed again. "I've got to tell someone, haven't I?" he said. "And at least you understand how much I wanted to travel out there in the System. I'm sick of being tied down to one measly little planetoid when there's a Universe out there to explore."

"There's Virtual Reality," she pointed out.

"That's not good enough and you know that as well as I do," he snapped. "A whole new race, Shari; I want to be one of the first to meet them. I have to get away!"

Shari considered her old friend; she had never seen him so determined or angry. And never before had they spoken so frankly, not even outside Galileo. It was as if his anger at not being allowed to travel off-world made him oblivious to the danger of anyone eavesdropping on them. She looked back up at the stars; one of those twinkling lights out there was TerraNova. Another might even be the Seti starship.

And among those lights she was suddenly sure was the father she had never believed was dead.

What I'm thinking is crazy, she told herself. Irresponsible, immature and definitely illegal…

She reached out to Kristas and made him look at her. She took a deep breath. If anyone had bugged the balcony then they had already said enough to get them into serious trouble; she might as well go the whole way.

"Kristas, let's leave."

Kristas stared at her as if she were mad. Which I very probably am, she realized.

"Leave Pasiphae?" he gasped. "But how?"

"You've travelled in a skimmer before to get to Amalthea," she reminded him.

"But I've never piloted one," he said. "And how are we going to get our hands on one anyway? This is the real world, Shari: get serious!"

Shari shook her head fiercely. "No, Kristas, I've just been condemned by the Board to spending the rest of my life filing and refiling lots of bureaucratic claptrap, and I do not want to 'get serious'."

Kristas remained silent, impressed by Shari's sudden determination, and allowed her to continue.

"I've had it with Pasiphae and its stupid rules and

regulations," she said. "I want to get out there, among the stars!"

"You're running away."

"Too right I'm running away!" she said.

Kristas paused for a moment, taking in what Shari had just told him. "It's hopeless, Shari," he said, although Shari had fired his own determination to escape. "Even if we did manage to find someone who would take us off-world, even if we were able to break into one of the spaceports and steal a skimmer, we'd never get through planetary security. There's a whole string of security ships and satellites circling the whole of Pasiphae..."

"I'm prepared to take the risk," she insisted. "I don't want to die an old woman, after working for years in the archives, knowing that I never once tried. Now, are you going to help me?"

Kristas regarded Shari with affection. It was a crazy idea, almost unheard of. If they were caught they stood the risk of being imprisoned, or being diagnosed as having personality disorders and forced to undergo corrective brain surgery. That was if they didn't get killed in the attempt.

And if they succeeded who knew what was out there for them? Neither of them had been to Terra-Nova, or the Home Planet before, and they would certainly never be allowed to return to Pasiphae. They would be leaving all their fellow students behind, all that they knew and felt familiar with. It was a huge leap into the unknown.

"Are you with me, Kristas?" Shari demanded.

Kristas nodded. "I'm with you."

Shari beamed and kissed him on the cheek. "Thank you."

"But where do we start?" Kristas asked, for once the practical one of them.

Shari looked out over the balcony, not at the night sky this time, but towards a rocky ridge on the horizon, on which a few dim lights glimmered. She remembered the stories of the Misfits who had chosen to drop out of Pasiphaean society and eke out a precarious existence in the planetoid's Wastelands.

"The Misfits will know," she told Kristas.

"They're thieves and beggars at best," he said, shocked at the suggestion.

"And that's what we are now," Shari reminded him. "Tomorrow morning we head out for Shanty-Land!"

Cruse

Kristas glowered at Shari. "I must be mad to let you talk me into this," he said through gritted teeth.

Shari grinned with a pleasure she certainly didn't feel, and slapped him amicably on the back.

"Then that makes two of us, doesn't it?" she said and stopped to massage her aching feet. They had been travelling on foot for almost an hour now, along uneven rocky and rubble-strewn paths: the surface of Pasiphae, outside the smooth metal and plastic walkways of Galileo, made for heavy and uncomfortable walking. In fact the only person who seemed to be enjoying the trek was Doob, who scampered on eagerly ahead, rooting about amongst the crevices of the rocks in search of the odd insect or scrub of plant.

Shari shivered. They were approaching that part of the planetoid which always had its face turned away from the artificial sun. It was deathly cold. All around them lay the hulks of burnt-out machines, abandoned when they had outlived their usefulness.

The Wastelands of Pasiphae were little more than an industrial junkyard filled with the discarded remains of the mighty engines which had once been used to transform the bleak and airless surface of this satellite into a planet on which human beings could survive. In the darkness the machines towered above Shari and Kristas, casting threatening shadows over the tortured and furrowed landscape.

ShantyLand lay beyond Rubble Mountain, which had been made from the waste and clinker left over from the terraforming of Pasiphae. Nestled in a small crater at the foot of the mountain, it was protected on all sides by steep and treacherous cliffs.

It was a widely known fact that drop-outs from Pasiphaean society had come out into the Wasteland and set up a group of small independent communities. Few Pasiphaeans, however, showed any interest in the inhabitants of the Wasteland. When they were mentioned it was more likely as a threat to recalcitrant children who refused to go to bed, than as a viable alternative to the ordered and comfortable life enjoyed in Galileo and Pasiphae's other towns.

Officially, of course, ShantyLand didn't exist; after all, for the System to recognize its existence would be to call into question its claim that all Pasiphaeans were supremely contented with their lot. So a sort of unhappy but expedient truce had sprung up between the Government and the people of ShantyLand: the Government didn't hound the ShantyLanders, and they, in their turn, didn't make their presence felt in Galileo and foment discontent amongst the Pasiphaeans.

Shari had always secretly admired the Misfits who had come out here. For her they represented a break from hated authority and regimentation, and she often idly wondered if those friends of hers from the Academy who had suddenly disappeared had, in fact, ended up here.

The Board, of course, simply replied to those courageous enough to ask that they had been relocated to other towns. Rumour had it that several eminent scientists, disillusioned with the restrictions the System placed on their researches, lived here, along with all the free-thinkers for whom the System's regime was anathema. Of course, that also meant that many of the ShantyLanders also comprised of drop-outs, and the criminal classes, whose existence the Board also seldom, if ever, recognized.

"I get the feeling that we're being watched all the time," said Kristas, as he felt the hairs on his neck rise.

"That's unlikely," said Shari as she looked around her nervously. "The Board's spy-cameras don't come out this far. It's only when we're in Galileo that there's the possibility of them dropping in on us."

"That's not what I meant," said Kristas. "I wasn't talking about electronic eyes..."

He looked around him. Behind them the lights of Galileo winked invitingly and warmly in the distance. "We could have been followed, you know."

"Who'd want to follow us out here?" Shari asked. "We're not doing anything that's illegal either."

"Mixing with thieves and criminals isn't illegal then?" asked Kristas sarcastically.

"We haven't mixed with them yet," she replied cheerfully. "A journey to ShantyLand isn't exactly advised by the Board, but it's not forbidden. Sometimes I get the idea that the Board are pleased when discontents like us leave Galileo for ShantyLand. At least that way they don't have to go to the trouble of getting rid of us."

Kristas looked nervously at her. "'Getting rid' of us? Do you believe the rumours?"

"That Donovan Trueheart's security forces kill anyone caught querying the System?" she said, and shrugged. "I really don't know for sure. But you know as well as I do, Kristas, that people have vanished over the years. Academicians like ourselves ... I heard that there was a big fuss about nine years ago, when six Academicians simply vanished into thin air."

Kristas nodded: the story had become almost

apocryphal amongst the students at the Academy. "Mad Marla," he said. "The Board said she'd been showing severe personality disorders for several months. Had this idea that all the knowledge of the last few centuries was a bad thing and that we'd all be better off living on Home Planet. And then she just ran off, along with five of her friends..."

"Not without wiping half of the info-disks in the Academy library first," Shari reminded him.

Kristas nodded. "That always struck me as odd ..." he said.

"Odd?"

"Well, OK, Mad Marla wiped the disks, that's understandable if she was as insane as the Board said she was," he continued. "But I would have thought that the Board would at the very least have back-up copies of the disks..."

"And they haven't?"

Kristas nodded. "I noticed it when I was doing some background for a translation of a technical paper. All records of biological research over the past hundred years are non-existent. Just as if someone wanted to hide something."

"Which is exactly what they did, with the Seti," Shari concluded.

"But why biological research?" asked Kristas. "And there was something else too – or rather there wasn't something else..."

"What?"

"Not one mention of Home Planet, or Earth, or whatever you want to call it," he said. "It's as if they want to deny its existence."

Shari chuckled wryly. "Well, here's something whose existence I'd like to deny..."

Ahead of them lay the slag hills at the foot of Rubble Mountain; even Doob forsook her curiosity and clambered back into Shari's arms. There was a distinct smell of sulphur in the air which made Kristas gag.

"How can the ShantyLanders live in these conditions?" he asked, recalling the warm and antiseptically clean walkways of Galileo.

"Looks like they value their freedom more than their comfort," said Shari philosophically, even though the smell was disgusting to her too. "Now c'mon!"

A sort of narrow pathway had been carved out of the side of Rubble Mountain and it curved steadily around the slag hill, leading finally down into Shanty-Land itself. With a sigh they set off on the pathway, unaware that only a few metres away from them, hidden behind one of the discarded terraforming machines, a figure was watching them.

Silhouetted against the sky, the figure was about six feet tall. Even in the darkness he seemed immensely powerful and threatening. He laughed scornfully at the departing figures of Shari and Kristas, and then silently followed them down into ShantyLand...

About thirty minutes later Shari and Kristas had reached the floor of the crater. Here on the crater's rim there was little evidence of human life. A few stone huts were dotted here and there, their walls covered with graffiti, but otherwise the place might have been a ghost town. They were on the outskirts of ShantyLand, Shari realized: they would have to walk much further towards the centre of the crater before they came across any other human beings.

As they trudged on, Doob began to tremble gently in Shari's arms. Shari cooed softly to her, but the little chimp still continued to whimper. Her eyes darted here and there as if trying to see something in the shadows.

"What's wrong with her?" Kristas asked. He was feeling distinctly uneasy too, unable to shake off the nagging suspicion that they were being watched by someone – or something.

Shari shrugged, determined not to let her own nervousness show. "She doesn't like this place," she said, trying to sound casual. "And let's face it, who in their right mind would? I've never seen such desolation."

As Shari and Kristas continued walking, the shadowy figure followed them, its feet never making a sound on the rocky and rubble-strewn ground.

Soon the desolate wasteland of the outer rim of the crater gave way to rows of stone and mud huts, lining rough dirt tracks which criss-crossed each other in a disordered and haphazard fashion. Shari and Kristas looked on in disgust: never in their cosy well-provided lives had they ever imagined such squalor before.

The "streets" were lined with every imaginable form of rubbish, and a rancid, fetid smell hung over the whole area, a stink so powerful that it could almost be touched.

Outside some of the dilapidated huts small fires burned, and around these sat groups of people, huddled together for warmth in the cold night air. They were dressed in rags and through the holes in their clothes Shari could make out their skeletal frames. Clearly these people were wildly under-nourished: she wondered just how they scavenged a living out here in the Wastelands where the only animals to be had for food were those domestic pets which had escaped from Galileo. She shuddered as she remembered those rumours, which she had once dismissed as sensationalist, of the Misfits practising cannibalism.

Well, it's now or never, Shari thought, and handed the now-silent Doob over to Kristas. She stepped forward towards the nearest group.

"Er ... hullo ..." she began uncertainly.

A few members of the group turned their heads slowly towards her. They looked at her through unblinking and uncaring eyes, considering her for a moment, before turning back towards the fire.

"It's no use," whispered Kristas, who had come up beside her. "They're drugged out of their minds. You won't get any sense out of them while they're in that condition."

"How can they ...?" Shari's voice trailed off. She'd heard about drug abuse in the 20th and 21st centuries, but had thought that the practice had been stamped out when the System government had been established. After all, the System was supposed to provide its citizens with every pleasure and diversion they could want, wasn't it? Why would people want to seek refuge and oblivion in drugs?

Kristas shrugged. "Maybe it's the only freedom they can have," he suggested grimly. "Their only escape from the System."

"You can't mean that," she retorted. "If these were the only people who lived in ShantyLand then do you think I'd have come here? What about all the others who they say have moved out here ... the scientists, the engineers, even the disillusioned administrators?"

Kristas shook his head despondently. "Maybe they didn't really come here. Maybe it was just a story after all ... like Mad Marla and her friends..."

Shari turned angrily on him. "And ShantyLand is just a 'story' too, is it? The System refuses to acknowledge that this place exists even though it's practically on our doorstep, but every single Galilean knows that it's here! And we're here, aren't we? Or maybe you're just too scared to go after your dream,

Kristas? Maybe you don't want to make your fantasy real, after all?"

Shari had struck a raw nerve. Kristas had had many dreams in his eighteen years: somehow the dream had always been more attractive than the reality.

"You're talking about my fantasy?" he snapped defensively. "Then what about yours?"

"What d'you mean?"

"Your father," he said. "Do you really believe he's alive after all these years?" Kristas bit his lip: he knew he'd gone too far. An awkward silence followed. Finally he said: "I'm sorry."

"Forget it," Shari said, although clearly Kristas too had touched on a raw nerve. She sniffed, and looked around her. "We're not going to find any help here," she said practically. "Let's move on."

They took a turning down what they supposed to be just another alleyway. After they had walked for several minutes they realized that they had walked into a darkened cul-de-sac. There was no sign of any life here, and tottering and shadowy buildings surrounded them on three sides. In Shari's arms Doob began to whimper again.

"Let's go back," said Kristas nervously. "There's nothing here for us."

Shari agreed and they turned to walk off in the direction they had come from. And then they stopped dead.

Standing in front of them were three sallow but

muscular youths. The oldest of them must have been only twelve or thirteen, but his eyes betrayed the hardness and cruelty that came from living most of his life in ShantyLand. He grinned at Shari and Kristas, revealing chipped and blackened teeth.

"Well, well, well," he sneered. "Look what we've got here, lads ..." His two companions chuckled menacingly and approached Shari and Kristas.

"Er ... hello ..." muttered Shari as she and Kristas automatically stepped back into the shadows.

"Who do you think they are?" asked one of the other two.

"Galileans," said the older boy, who was obviously their leader. He walked up to Shari and felt the fine material of her tunic, as Doob leapt out of her mistress's arms and ran off into the shadows. "Rich Galileans too, by the feel of this," he continued, and allowed his hand to remain just a little too long on Shari.

Kristas grabbed his hand and flung it roughly off Shari. "Leave her alone!" he said.

The boy laughed. "Sez who?" he asked, and from out of his own ragged tunic whipped out a knife. He held it at Kristas's throat.

"Look, leave us alone," said Shari. "We've done you no harm."

"Mebbe we don't want to leave you alone," he said. "Isn't that right, lads?"

His companions mumbled their agreement, and

advanced on Shari. She stepped back, looking sideways to where Kristas had been pressed up against the wall. There was no doubt that the boy would slit his throat without a second's thought, unless...

Like lightning she leapt on the boy, throwing her arm around his neck and dragging him away from Kristas. The knife fell clattering onto the rocky ground, and Kristas dived to pick it up.

He was too late. One of the boy's two companions rammed his foot down on Kristas's outstretched hand. As Kristas rolled over, yelping with pain, his attacker grabbed the knife, and waved it menacingly at him.

Meanwhile the other two had grabbed Shari, who struggled vainly in their iron grasp. She looked on, wide-eyed in terror, as the leader of the gang ripped open the front of her tunic.

This is Pasiphae, she kept on telling herself. This isn't supposed to happen! Why doesn't the System come to our rescue?

Shari had misjudged the boy's motives. He wasn't interested in her, but in the leather wallet she had been carrying in her tunic. He whipped the wallet out and his eyes gleamed with greed.

"How much?" asked the one who was still holding the struggling Shari.

"Enough," he said. "Enough to buy food for the next month or so..."

"What do we do about these two?" asked the thug who was still covering Kristas with his knife. "If we let them go back to Galileo they're bound to tell the System..."

The leader looked casually over at Kristas, and then back at Shari. "Kill them," he said evenly.

"It'll be a pleasure, boss," he said and raised his knife ready to plunge it deep down into Kristas's chest.

Suddenly a booted foot smashed into his face, knocking out several of his already decaying teeth. The force of the blow threw him off Kristas and he fell to the ground with a bone-crunching *thud!*

The stranger had appeared from seemingly out of nowhere. He leapt on Kristas's attacker, punching him in the face, and then rose to turn on the other two thugs. Cowards to a man, they released Shari and ran off into the night.

The stranger turned to the third boy, who was painfully crawling to his feet.

"You – get out of here too," the stranger said, "before I decide to get rough."

The stranger booted the thug in the backside, and laughed as he ran off after his two companions. The stranger turned and looked down at Shari and Kristas with cynical, all-appraising eyes. He was about six feet tall, firm and muscular, and appeared to be about eight or nine years older than Shari and Kristas.

He was dressed in an old leather waistcoat and trousers, and from the belt about his waist hung all manner of objects – from tools such as spanners to something which Kristas thought looked suspiciously like the guns he had seen in the sensationalist vid-disks he had seen when Shari hadn't been watching.

His long black hair was tied back in a ponytail and looked as though it hadn't been washed for days. His hair framed a rough face which, although not attractive by Galilean standards, still had a certain rugged handsomeness to it.

Shari and Kristas glanced at each other, unsure what to do next. In Shari's arms, Doob started to chitter happily, and looked curiously at the stranger.

Finally Shari spoke: "Er . . . thank you. . ."

The stranger continued to look at them for several long and unpleasant seconds. Finally the corners of his mouth turned up in a condescending smirk, and he nodded an acknowledgement.

"It was nothing," he muttered. His voice was dark and surly. "You have to be careful in ShantyLand. There are lots of hungry people out here." He looked in the direction in which the muggers had run off. "Still the credits they took from you will stop their bellies rumbling for a while, I'll wager. What they don't spend on drugs, that is."

"You saved our lives back there," Kristas said gratefully.

"That's right," said the stranger. His voice betrayed no emotion whatsoever. "I did, didn't I?"

"I guess you'd like to know who we are and what we're doing here," Shari continued awkwardly.

She'd never been in the position of having to thank anyone for saving her life before, and there was also something rather off-putting about this taciturn figure.

"I already know," said the man. "A couple of rich kids, come down to ShantyLand to slum it for a thrill. We get lots of 'em." He glared sinisterly at Shari and Kristas. "Some of them even make it back to Galileo alive…"

By Shari's side Kristas gulped, but Shari decided that she was not going to let herself be intimidated by the stranger.

"We're not rich kids," she began.

"You're from Galileo," the man stated simply. "Compared to the ShantyLanders that makes you rich."

You all choose to drop out of society and live in ShantyLand, was what Shari wanted to say. It's not our fault that we don't scavenge and rob and kill for food like you Misfits do!

What she did say was: "We're not here slumming it for kicks!"

"Oh, you're not now, are you?" The stranger smiled. Shari's sudden change of manner amused rather than intimidated him.

"We're looking for someone who can help us…"

The man raised an interested eyebrow but said nothing.

"We're looking for people who can get us off Pasiphae," Kristas volunteered.

"And you think you can find that sort of help here?" the man asked mockingly.

"We know that ShantyLand isn't just made up of druggies and crooks," Shari replied, staring directly at the stranger and making it quite plain what class she thought he belonged to. "There are students out here who have escaped from the Academy. Scientists, engineers, people of influence, they've all come here..."

The stranger nodded. "That's true," he said.

Damn him! cursed Kristas. Why won't he answer in anything more than monosyllables?

Shari, however, frowned, realizing the game the stranger was playing with them. He was cleverly drawing out from her and Kristas as much information as he could, without volunteering anything about himself. In this way he would have the advantage over them.

For all his intimidating ways he's as wary of us as we are of him, she suddenly understood. Well, two can play at that game!

Shari strode boldly up to the stranger, even as the more cautious Kristas tried to hold her back.

"My name's Shari Sharifi," she announced coolly. "And this is Kristas Chernenko." She looked defiantly into the stranger's eyes. "And who are you?"

"They call me Cruse around here," he said, and chuckled. There was something about this plucky young girl which he rather liked. He paused, as if sizing her up, and then continued. "But if you want help in getting off-world, you've come to the wrong place."

Kristas's face fell, but Shari wasn't so easily dissuaded.

"You've seen the ShantyLanders," he said in response to her unspoken question. "Junkies and petty crooks. You think they could help you? They're more concerned with getting their next fix than interplanetary physics."

Shari hesitated. "What about the scientists who've come out here?" she asked, doubtfully. "The engineers and physicists who've left the Academy could help us."

Cruse laughed, a long patronizing laugh. "You think people like that would remain for long in ShantyLand? Look around you – who in their right minds would want to stay here? They've all gone, Shari – you've arrived too late!"

Shari glanced briefly at Kristas, who was looking distinctly ill-at-ease. Had their daring escapade been for nothing? She turned back to Cruse.

"Then we'll just have to find them," she said defiantly. "Where have they gone to?"

"To Earth," Cruse said simply.

"To the Home Planet?" gasped Kristas, hardly noticing in his disbelief that Cruse had used the planet's old name. The Home Planet had been declared off-limits for almost a century now. "It can still support life?"

"That's right," said Cruse. "Oh, the ozone layer's been near blasted away, and you'll be lucky to find fresh water, or arable soil. But there's life there, all right, away from the prying eyes of the System..."

"But how did they get there?" asked Shari.

Cruse laughed again. "How do you think? They were taken there."

"*You* took them there?" Somehow the rough and unshaven man in front of them didn't seem to be the sort of material space pilots were made of. Cruse didn't reply, and merely continued to smirk.

"Graduated from the Academy nine years ago," Cruse volunteered. "Top grades in physics and engineering science. Spent my first year ferrying people between Pasiphae and the mines on Jupiter; until I got wise to the ways of the System, that is."

Kristas stepped forward, determined not to be intimidated by the older man. "If you're a graduate from the Academy, why haven't we heard of you?" he asked reasonably.

Cruse laughed scornfully, and shook his head. Although he was only a few years older than Kristas and Shari it was obvious that he regarded them as little more than children. He seemed to relax and sat down on a pile of rubble.

"I was probably wiped from all System records the minute I died," he chuckled. "It wouldn't do for it to be officially known that some of Pasiphae's citizens didn't actually like the way the System runs and got killed for it.''

"Dead?" asked Kristas in wonderment. "Killed?"

"That's right," said Cruse and laughed bitterly. "The corpse that walked away, that's me." He rolled up his shirt and showed them the vicious scar that ran down his right-hand side. "Marla and the others weren't so lucky."

"Mad Marla?" asked Kristas, and gasped as Cruse grabbed him by the throat.

"Don't you ever call her by that name again!" he barked, before relaxing his grip on the boy.

"The Board knew that they couldn't keep secret what happened to Marla," he continued. "So they invented the story that she was mad and one day she mysteriously vanished, along with her friends; never to be spoken of again, except in naughty whispers." He shook his head, and for just a moment Shari could detect a touch of genuine sorrow in Cruse's voice. "But there was nothing mad about Marla. All she wanted was her freedom."

"I'm sorry," said Shari. "Kristas didn't mean to upset you..."

"Forget I mentioned it," he said gruffly.

Shari decided that there was an urgent need to change the subject.

"Can you take us to the Home Planet – I mean, Earth," asked Shari.

"You're just another couple of kids who feel hemmed in by the System," Cruse said. "A couple of years and you'll get used to it like anyone else."

Shari looked defiantly at Cruse, aware that he was testing their resolve.

"No we won't," she declared. "There's no way that I'm going to settle down to a life as a bureaucrat. Besides, there's my father..."

Cruse's manner changed when she told him about her father. There was a new tone of respect in his voice, and he suddenly became much more interested in Shari and Kristas.

"I knew him," he said and, in response to Shari's wide-eyed look of amazement, added: "I studied under him for a year when I was at the Academy. He was a brilliant physicist, one of the leaders in tachyon technology."

Tachyon technology? Shari and Kristas looked blankly at each other, and were about to pursue the matter further when Cruse turned to Kristas.

"And you – why do you want to leave the System?" he asked. It was clear that he didn't think the sensitive and idealistic Kristas was the sort of person to take part in a daring escape from Pasiphae.

Kristas looked askance. "I have my reasons ..." he said. "You wouldn't understand them." He glanced up; in the night sky a particularly brilliant shooting star was streaking through the darkness.

Cruse chuckled; he was a master of interpreting

body language, and Kristas's involuntary movement had given him away.

"They'll be here soon," he said casually, and both Kristas and Shari looked sharply at him. "The Seti, of course," he answered in response to their unasked question.

"How do you know about them?" Kristas demanded, and even though they were in the open air, far away from the Board's space cameras he found that he was whispering. "No one's supposed to know."

"I fly to Mars and Earth, remember?" he said. "You can't help but know. Why do you think no one's been allowed off-world for the past few years?"

"We were told that there was danger of contracting space plague," said Kristas.

"And you believed that?" he asked.

"Of course not," said Kristas and then added: "Well, at first we did..."

Cruse shook his head.

"Mankind's first contact with a totally alien species has thrown the whole of the System into a panic," he said. "It doesn't fit into their precise and ordered little world. They don't know whether to greet the Seti with open arms or shoot them down before they get too close.

"The Seti are hundreds of times more advanced than we are."

"You don't know that," said Shari.

"They've travelled thousands of light years to get

here," he said. "Earth technology is interplanetary: it can take us as far as Pluto and then that's it. After that our power sources run out and pack up. But the Seti have mastered interstellar travel, and who knows what else? In their eyes we're probably little more than primitives."

Shari remembered her studies of ancient Earth history. She recalled the fate of the Aborigines of Australia, or the Indians of North America, when the more "civilized" Europeans had landed on their continents. Both races had been exploited and abused almost to extinction. Who was to say that that wasn't the fate the Seti had in store for them?

"But if they're as civilized as you say they are," said Kristas, "then surely they've left all that barbarism behind them?"

Cruse looked scornfully at Kristas, and then nodded to Shari.

"Does your friend always live in his own little dream world?" he asked contemptuously. "Mobs for and against the Seti are rioting in the streets of New Canberra," he reminded Kristas. "Donovan Trueheart and his EarthLifers Party are calling for the Seti to be nuked out of existence before they even reach the Asteroid Belt ... And you both want to leave Pasiphae for that mess?"

Shari and Kristas looked uncertainly at each other. For a moment the peaceful and well-organized, if dull, life they had led here suddenly became strangely attractive. Finally Shari looked Cruse in the eye.

"We want to go," she said with determination.

"Then you're both bigger fools than even I had taken you for," Cruse said, but Shari could detect a glint of admiration in his dark eyes.

"Will you take us?" she asked.

Cruse considered the two for a moment. The girl was fine, he decided; beneath her pretty and delicate exterior there was a heart of steel. Determined, fiery and self-willed she would prove to be a useful companion in a tight spot. However, he wasn't so sure about Kristas: he was a dreamer and Cruse doubted whether he would survive for more than a day outside the borders of Galileo.

He shrugged philosophically; their welfare wasn't his prime concern, he realized. In the end it all came down to one thing.

"It'll cost you," he said.

"We have money," said Kristas.

"You *had* money," Cruse corrected him. "You were mugged, remember?"

"We have more credits back in Galileo," Shari said quickly.

Cruse took a pencil and a scrap of paper out of his pouch, and scribbled down some figures. He handed the paper to Shari.

"That's my price," he said. "Make sure that credits are transferred into that numbered account by first light tomorrow. And get ready to leave. I'll contact you."

"You don't know where we live in Galileo," Kristas pointed out.

"System records," Cruse said. "It won't be the first time I've hacked into them. I did it once before – nine years ago..."

Shari frowned suspiciously. "And what guarantee do we have that you'll keep your side of the bargain?"

"You've no guarantee," Cruse replied, more amused than affronted by Shari's distrust. "But if you don't trust me then you're going to be no use to me on the flight off-world, are you?"

"But..."

"It's up to you, Shari," Cruse said. "Do you really want to leave Pasiphae? Or is it just a dream? Do you want to risk putting all your credits into that bank account? Or do you want to spend the rest of your life wondering what might have happened if, just for once, you had done what you really wanted to?"

And with that Cruse turned and ran off, vanishing into the shadows of ShantyLand. Shari and Kristas stared after him for a while, before turning to each other. They needed to say nothing: while neither of them completely trusted Cruse, each of them had reached the same decision.

Kristas looked up at that strange shooting star which seemed to be dominating the entire sky.

"It will mean that there's no going back, Shari," he said.

Shari nodded. "There's just one thing that's worrying me," she admitted.

"And what's that?"

"How am I going to break the news to Kili?"

As Shari and Kristas turned back and began the long trek back to Galileo, neither of them noticed the figure observing them, hidden behind a pile of forgotten rubble.

He was tall and thin and was leaning on a cane. A smile broke on his wizened features and he chuckled sagely to himself.

Shari and Kristas, even Cruse, might not know it but everything was going according to plan. He looked up into the sky at the shooting star which was speeding past Pasiphae.

Soon, he realized, the Seti's mission would be over, a mission that would result in the death of an entire species.

He felt a pudgy hand tugging at his sleeve, and looked down at the fat little form of Jared, Shari and Kristas's fellow student.

"Did I do well, my Lord?" Jared oozed.

The old man smiled. "You did very well, Jared, my boy," he said.

"I knew you'd be interested," Jared said. "The moment I saw them talking together I knew that they were up to something. That's why I came and told you, that's why we followed them tonight..."

The old man stroked his chin thoughtfully. "I hadn't expected them to meet up with Cruse so soon," he said to himself. "I may have to change my plans slightly..."

"Your plans, my Lord?" asked Jared.

"Just the whims of an old, old man," his companion said. "Nothing for someone like you to be worried about."

Jared grunted, and rubbed his hands gleefully. "Will the Board be informed?" he asked eagerly, already thinking up numerous sadistic punishments for Shari and Kristas.

"Entering ShantyLand isn't a crime, Jared."

"No, but consorting with rebels and criminals is," he replied with relish. "Will you tell the Board? Will you tell Lord Trueheart?"

The old man chuckled. "Somehow I think Donovan Trueheart has more important things to concern himself with than an errant girl and her boyfriend."

"He's not her boyfriend," Jared said sulkily. "They told me. I thought he was because they're always together and she's always refusing to go out with me..."

And of course it has nothing to do with the fact that you're a stinking and abhorrent piece of slime, the old man thought.

"No, I shall not tell the Board," said the old man, and Jared frowned.

"But why not?" he whined. "They deserve to be punished. I told you about them, I brought you here tonight."

"For which you shall be rewarded, Jared," the old man said.

"I should think so," said Jared. "After all my father's one of the chief administrators – if he were to find out that you were hiding something from the Board..."

The old man laughed. "Why, I do believe you're threatening me, Jared!"

Jared sulked, but the old man continued to laugh. "And what else have you found out about Shari and Kristas?" he asked. "The mechanical eyes and ears of the System cannot be everywhere; that is why we also rely on people like you."

Jared thought hard. "They keep on going on about the..." he struggled to recall the unfamiliar word. "... the Seti."

"*The Seti?*" the old man asked. "What do *you* know about the Seti?"

Jared was taken aback by his companion's abrupt change of manner. The old man he previously regarded as a soft touch now suddenly seemed very threatening indeed.

"Not a lot," he admitted. "Kristas was talking some

nonsense about creatures from outer space. Little green men with three heads, that sort of thing."

"Only one head," the old man muttered to himself, "and certainly not green."

"What?" asked Jared. The old man was shaking his head.

"You shouldn't have known about that, Jared," he said. "I paid you to spy on Shari and Kristas when they were at the Academy and when my other agent was unable to..."

"Your other agent?" asked Jared. This was the first time he had heard his aged employer talk of someone else snooping on Shari and Kristas.

"And now you have learnt of the Seti ..." There was a sad note of finality in his voice.

Jared was suddenly very frightened. "I promise I won't tell a soul," he said nervously.

"Ah, but can I believe that, when you betray your own friends so easily?" the old man asked rhetorically. "You might even tell your father..."

"On my life, I swear I won't!"

"There are already rumours and discontent on TerraNova," he said. "As an official of the System I cannot allow news of the Seti's existence to spread to Pasiphae ... And in my other – far greater – capacity, I cannot allow anything to stop the Seti from reaching Home Planet, or prevent Shari and Kristas from meeting them there."

"Your greater capacity? I don't understand..."

"And I'm afraid, Jared, you will never get the opportunity to understand."

In one swift and fluid movement the old man whipped a gun out of his jacket, and shot Jared in the stomach. The fat boy didn't have time to cry out and slammed to the rocky ground.

The old man replaced his gun and shook his head. It was so sad to kill the young, he reflected, even someone as odious and treacherous as Jared. His parents would have to be killed as well, he recognized; otherwise they might start to query their son's disappearance, and that would never do.

It was even sadder that he had to use the ways of the System to ensure silence. Even though he was a high-ranking official of the System, such killing wasn't in the old man's nature. But, he reminded himself, sometimes out of a necessary evil a greater good could arise. That still didn't make it any easier, he reflected bitterly.

The old man walked way, leaving Jared's corpse behind. It wasn't left undisturbed for long however. The three thugs who had earlier attacked Shari and Kristas approached the still warm body.

As Cruse had predicted, the credits they had stolen from Shari would be spent on drugs. And they still had to find credits with which to buy food. They fell onto Jared's body, stripping it of its clothes, and searching through his pockets for credits and anything else they could use to trade for food and more drugs.

Such was the everyday way of life in ShantyLand.

Two Months to Earth

As the egg-shaped spacecraft sped past Jupiter, few eyes turned to look at the mighty gas giant and its great red spot. The masters of this craft were concerned with much weightier matters, of which the awe-inspiring splendour of the largest planet in the Solar System was not one.

Besides, the appreciation of beauty was for the young, and the race which had fashioned this craft were older even than the ancient planet to which they were heading.

However, the other creatures who inhabited the spacecraft paused from their labours to gaze in wonder at the giant yellow sphere. They chittered and chuckled to each other and smiled. The planet seemed strangely familiar to them, as if sighting it had reawoken in them some long-lost race memory. Or perhaps it was because they somehow sensed the presence on that world and its satellites of thinking and feeling creatures like themselves.

The creatures turned as they heard an angry snarl from behind them. With its eyes blazing red and acidic saliva dripping from its powerful jaws, one of their masters was ordering them away from the viewports. With submissive whimpers the small two-legged hairy creatures scurried back to work.

The creature who had given the orders paused and looked out through the viewport. This creature was young, barely a few hundred years old, and this was its first time in space; it still had time to appreciate the wonders of the Universe.

It marvelled at the sheer determination and ingenuity of the human beings who had left their own planet to set up colonies and industries on other worlds. It had taken the Seti many hundreds of thousands of years to evolve into the creatures they now were and then to make the great leap into space. Yet it had taken human beings a mere five thousand years to raise themselves up from out of the primeval slime of their home planet and launch themselves amongst the stars.

That was surely an achievement worth celebrating, thought the creature, and then sharply rebuked itself. Sentimentality had no place in the Seti's mission, it reminded itself, not if that mission had to be carried out with the precision and accuracy it demanded.

After all, sentimentality was hardly fitting when the purpose of the Seti's mission was nothing less than the ruthless extermination of an entire species. It only hoped the humans on the Earth would realize it was for their own good...

Escape!

"I don't trust him, Shari," said Kristas the following morning as they sat on Shari's bed at the Academy.

"We don't have any choice," she replied, keeping her voice low, even though the raucous music from her bedside entertainment console was purposely drowning out their voices. It was still early and most of her fellow students weren't yet awake, but they couldn't afford to be too careful. What they were planning was tantamount to treason, and if they were discovered now there was no telling what punishment would be meted out to them by the Board.

She continued putting a few items of sentimental value into a rucksack: pictures of her father, some small fossils from Earth, a vid-disk on the dinosaurs which Kili had given her when she was small.

"Cruse is the only person who might be able to help me track down my father..."

"And just how do you make that out?"

"He knew Mad Marla, remember ... There've always been stories about her."

"Put about by the Board, you mean."

"No, the other stories that we're not supposed to know about. That she was about to make a stand against the entire System. And that when she vanished—"

"—or was killed if we believe Cruse."

"Someone escaped and survived out there in ShantyLand, helping others to escape off-world."

"I still don't like it ... We've no guarantee he'll keep his side of the bargain once he's got his hands on your credits."

Shari took hold of Kristas's shoulders and forced him to look at her. "He's also the only chance either of us will ever have of getting off-world, Kristas," she said, almost imploringly. "What Cruse said was right: if we don't try now we'll spend the rest of our lives regretting it!"

Kristas still hesitated until Shari delivered her *coup de grâce*: "Think of the Seti, Kristas! The very first contact between human beings and a completely alien race. Creatures that no one in the whole of human history has ever encountered before! We can't afford to miss out on that opportunity!"

Kristas nodded. "You're right, of course," he admitted. "But that still doesn't make me any happier having to deal with him . . . Did you arrange the credit transfer?"

Shari nodded. "I cleared out my stipend from the Board as soon as I woke up this morning," she said. "By now there should be ten thousand credits sitting in Cruse's mysterious numbered account."

"Won't the Board be suspicious?"

Shari shook her head. "Remember I'm being transferred to the other side of the planet," she said. "What could be more natural than me taking out my credits ready to put them into a brand-new account?"

"So all we have to do now is wait for him to contact us," said Kristas in a voice which suggested that he doubted they would ever see the mercenary, or Shari's credits, again.

"I trust him even if you don't," Shari said reprovingly.

"Yes," said Kristas gloomily, "to the tune of ten thousand credits."

Shari glanced over at her pet chimp. "And so did Doob, and that's good enough for me."

Kristas laughed at the little chimp's antics, and wondered what Cruse's reaction would be when he discovered that Shari was determined to take Doob along with her. Somehow he couldn't see Cruse being as sentimental over the animal as he and Shari were.

The vid-phone by Shari's bed beeped and she operated the pick-up control. The screen flared into life but there was no picture, just a hazy blur of static: whoever was calling had decided that he didn't want to be seen on an open channel. Shari and Kristas looked anxiously at each other: could it be Cruse contacting them as promised?

"Hello? Who's there?"

There was a pause, before the voice at the other end spoke up. Neither of them recognized it; if it was indeed Cruse's voice then it must have been electronically altered. Whoever was on the other line was taking no chances of being discovered.

"Miss Sharifi ..." The voice was brusque and business-like.

"Yes ... Who is this?" asked Shari.

"Are you alone?" demanded the voice, without identifying itself.

"Apart from Kristas, yes," Shari replied, looking guiltily at Doob who had come up on the bed to join them in staring at the scrambled picture on the screen.

"Good. About the 'business' we discussed last night ... I've arranged your 'documents'," the voice continued before giving them an address. "Be there in thirty minutes." And then the screen went blank.

Perplexed, Shari and Kristas looked at each other;

the address was a large industrial site on the outskirts of Galileo, easily reached by hover-bus. It certainly didn't seem to be the sort of place from which to organize an escape from Pasiphae.

"What do we do?" asked Kristas, unsure whether the voice on the vid-phone had been Cruse's or not. Naturally cautious, he certainly wouldn't have been surprised if the Board had discovered their plans and were leading them into a trap.

"There's only one thing we can do," said Shari and grabbed her back pack and stood up. "We have to believe it was Cruse. Are you coming?"

Kristas shrugged his shoulders, succumbing to the inevitable. He picked Doob up in his arms and stood up, and they marched towards the door. The door swished open – and Kili was standing there, blocking their way.

"Oh ... er, hi, Kili," breezed Shari, wondering what the robot was doing at the Academy so early in the morning.

"I cannot allow you to go, Shari," the robot stated flatly.

"Go? Go where? We weren't going anywhere," Kristas lied.

"Apart from an early-morning stroll, that is," Shari added somewhat feebly.

"I cannot allow you to leave Pasiphae," the robot repeated. There was a new and slightly threatening tone in Kili's voice. "I overheard your conversation with that ... that reprobate."

"You've been spying on me!" Shari cried. "You've been listening in on my vid-phone!"

Kili clicked with embarrassment. "It's just as well that it was I," he said. "Because I was on the line no one else could listen in. Such as the Board.

"I am merely concerned for your welfare, Shari," Kili continued and then tut-tutted like an interfering old maiden aunt. "I can't have you falling in with the wrong sort now, can I? Whatever would your father say if he ever found out?"

"Leave my father out of this," Shari retorted furiously.

"I cannot leave your father out of it," Kili said meaningfully.

Shari frowned and looked suspiciously at her guardian: just how much did he know about her reasons for wanting to leave Pasiphae? Kili often behaved like a doddery but much-loved family retainer, but there were times when she had suspected that he knew much more than he ever cared to reveal.

"Leaving Pasiphae is a criminal offence," Kili continued.

"So is eavesdropping on other people's conversations," she replied moodily.

"After your father, I took full responsibility for your upbringing," Kili reminded her. "My prime directive is to ensure your safety at all times. I am a robot, Shari, that order is programmed into my micro-circuits, and I cannot let you risk your life in this insane caper."

"Look, Shari, maybe Kili's right," said Kristas. "Maybe this isn't such a good idea after all."

Shari ignored him and considered Kili. The robot wouldn't hurt them, of that she was sure; but neither would it let them get past its two-and-a-half-ton bulk. That was the trouble with robots, she realized, they always played by the rules, while humans knew that sometimes a bit of cheating was called for to win the game.

Of course, that's it!

She looked slyly at Kili.

"Your prime directive is to make sure that I come to no harm, isn't that right, Kili? And that order cannot be overridden; you must always follow your prime directive?"

"You know I must, Shari," Kili's voice was softer, now that he thought Shari was being reasonable and seeing his point of view.

Shari stroked her chin thoughtfully; the angry glare in her eyes had been replaced by a mischievous gleam.

"So what would you do if I ignored your orders?" she asked. "What if I tried to escape?"

"I should have to stop you," he said.

"Lock me in my room like a naughty schoolgirl?" she asked, goading the robot on. "Restrain me?"

Kili sighed a mechanical sigh. "If it was necessary, yes," he admitted.

"But I'm a determined little human being, Kili, you've known me long enough to realize that," Shari continued. "I'd still keep on trying. Then what would you do?"

"Regrettably I would have no other course but to inform the Board," Kili said.

Gotcha! thought Shari, and even Kristas grinned as he guessed what was coming next.

"And then the Board would lock me up, maybe execute me!" she said triumphantly. "They still execute people for what they class as treason."

Kristas noticed that Kili didn't contradict Shari, even though the Board's official line was that executions were used only rarely and as only the severest form of punishment.

She looked defiantly at Kili. "And execution isn't very good for my well-being, now is it, Kili? So much for your prime directive!"

"Ah ..." said Kili, as he felt his logic circuits undergo the robotic equivalent of a crisis of faith.

"So you see, Kili," she said sweetly, and patted the robot affectionately on its chest plate, "if you don't let me pass, you fail your prime directive." She pretended to consider the matter. "In fact, there really is only one way in which you can carry out your prime directive…"

"There is?" Kili asked eagerly.

"Yup. You come with us. You're right, Kili, it's a dangerous universe out there, and a girl needs someone to protect her!"

She walked past the confused robot and out into the corridor. Kristas and Doob followed her.

Kili stood in the doorway, puzzling over Shari's argument. Deep down in his microchips he had the strongest feeling that he'd just been outwitted by an expert.

And a mere human being at that! he clicked to himself. But two can play at that game!

"Well, I suppose I must resign myself to the inevitable," he declared loudly, and stumped off after the departing humans.

It was still dark when Shari and her friends reached the industrial site where Cruse had arranged to meet them. Shari had never visited this part of Galileo before; indeed few Academicians were encouraged ever to leave Central Galileo. Now she knew why; her surroundings disgusted her.

A fetid smell hung over the entire area, the by-product of all the huge machines which, even at this early hour, were rumbling into action in the filthy factories which crisscrossed the whole place. Tall towers spewed forth black and acidic smoke, and in the gutters of the walkways ran rivers of slag and filth. Compared to the rest of Galileo, which was pristine in its metallic and plastic cleanliness, and landscaped with greenery transplanted from TerraNova and the Home Planet, this place was a vision of Hell. Even ShantyLand was preferable to this place.

They were huddled together in a tiny alleyway, away from the prying eyes of any Galileans on their way to work. As they wondered how they would meet Cruse in this great mass of people and sweat shops, Kristas peered at the tall buildings which seemed clouded in perpetual shadows.

"What do they do here?" he asked.

"It's like a giant refinery," said Shari. "The gases and minerals from Jupiter are processed here before being shipped back to TerraNova."

"But what for?"

Shari shrugged. She'd heard rumours of a mighty engineering project on TerraNova, but had always assumed that it was somehow connected with making habitable those areas of Mars which had still proved resistant to the Terraformers.

She glanced over at Kili, who was standing in the shadows, volunteering no information. He'd been silent on the entire journey here; if he hadn't been a robot and technically incapable of feelings Shari would have sworn that he'd been sulking.

"I hate this place," Kristas decided. This was the first time he had ever ventured out here too. "Did you see the look on the faces of those workers? It's confirmed what I always thought. I don't want to be a part of any society that treats people like mindless drones. No wonder so many people end up in ShantyLand."

"You and I are part of a privileged class, Kristas, members of the Academy," Shari reminded him. "I guess some people just aren't so lucky."

"I'm glad you've finally come to your senses and realized that," came a voice from behind them.

They all spun round to see Cruse standing in the shadows, where only a few seconds ago there had been no one. He was dressed in old black leather and a blaster hung in a holster at his side.

"Cruse! Where did you come from?" gasped Shari. The mercenary seemed to have appeared out of thin air, and, if anything, looked more dirty and dishevelled than usual.

Cruse grinned, revealing chipped and yellowed teeth. He opened his mouth to speak and then stopped. In a flash he grabbed his side gun and pointed it at Shari and her friends. They stepped back in terror.

"What is *that*?" he barked and pointed to Kili's tall and imposing figure in the shadows.

"It's only Kili," Kristas said simply, as the robot stepped out of the shadows. "You needn't be frightened, you know," he added sarcastically.

Cruse glared at the younger man. "What's it doing here?" he demanded.

"It's coming with us," Shari stated firmly. "And it's not an 'it', it's a 'he'."

Cruse looked at Shari as if she was mad, but also realized that it was pointless arguing with her.

"This is not a game which you can bring all your friends to, Shari," he reminded her. "We could end up getting killed." He looked scornfully at Kili. "I don't like this robot or any other. Not for nine years now, ever since Marla and the others died when a ServoRobot betrayed us. They're all the same; they're not to be trusted."

Kili's visual circuitry blazed violet with indignation. "I assure you I am a robot of my word!" he insisted.

Cruse looked at Kili through narrowed suspicious eyes. Yet there was something else in that look too that only the observant Kristas noticed: Cruse was *frightened* of Kili, and Kristas thought he knew the reason why.

For Cruse to have survived so long out in Shanty-Land he had to be a man who lived off his wits. He was a successful fighter, and part of the reason for his success was his ability to read his enemies' body language. The slightest movement, the least involuntary motion of the head, or flickering of the eyes, could give away an enemy's intentions and plans. Robots, however, have no body language, and Cruse was unable to tell what they were thinking of.

Kristas made a mental note to remember that: it could be useful later on.

Cruse strode up to Kili and looked up into the robot's impassive face.

"Designation!" he demanded.

Kili affected a yawning noise as if to say that he found Cruse a particularly annoying and troublesome specimen of homo sapiens. However, he replied: "Kilimanjaro."

"Model?"

"A Mark Seven ServoRobot of the CT002/4 line."

Cruse arched an interested eyebrow. "That old, eh? I thought that line had been discontinued and junked over a hundred years ago."

"Some of us do not belong on the junk-heap, no matter how old we may be," Kili said pompously, and even Cruse allowed himself a small chuckle.

By his side Shari looked at Cruse with new-found respect. She realized how little she and Kristas knew of the mercenary's background; neither of them had expected that he would be an expert in robotics as well.

"Offensive capability?"

"Nil. I am not empowered to harm humans."

"He even used to have trouble cooking the Sunday roast," offered Shari in an attempt to lighten up the conversation. Cruse glared at her.

"So you're going to be of no blasted use to us at all," Cruse decided angrily. "That is, if you're telling the truth, of course ..." He considered Kili's imposing seven-feet-high figure before asking: "Weight?"

"I assure you, sir, that that is none of your business!" Kili said with affronted dignity.

"Of course it's my blasted business!" Cruse snapped. "I didn't expect to be carrying a ruddy tin can all the way to TerraNova, did I? I'm going to have to make allowances for your weight!"

"Two and a half tons, if you must know," said Kili prissily. "I take it your transportation can carry my weight?" he added sarcastically.

"I don't have my own craft," Cruse said. "We're going to have to steal one."

Kili turned to Shari. "I have now become a criminal and a common thief!" he complained to her.

"It's all in a good cause, Kili," Shari whispered as Cruse made a rapid series of calculations. Suddenly he saw Doob who had been sitting there huddled at Kristas's feet. His face fell in a look of utter disbelief.

"And what is that?"

Shari suddenly felt very small indeed. However, she managed to maintain an air of dignity: "That is my pet chimp, Doob, and she's coming with us as well!"

Cruse raised his eyes heavenwards. "What am I running here? An escape attempt, or a ruddy family outing to see the Seti!"

"Not so loud!" Kristas said automatically. "No one's supposed to know about—" He stopped as he realized that all of them knew by now of the aliens' existence.

All of us except Kili, that is, he realized, and glanced over at the robot who had displayed neither curiosity nor surprise at hearing the name of the Seti mentioned.

"Might I be allowed to make a suggestion?" asked Kili.

"If you must, robot."

"Perhaps we ought to be going now," he said. "It will only be a matter of time before someone questions our presence here, I am sure."

"First bit of good sense I've heard all day," agreed Cruse, "and from a robot as well!"

"Where are we going to?" asked Kristas.

"Spaceport Five."

"But that's heavily guarded; we'd never get past security," he said, remembering the time when he had to fly from there to go to Amalthea. It was the strict border checks and security searches there that had first alerted Kristas to the fact that all might not be well in the System.

Cruse looked at Kristas as a haughty schoolteacher might to a particularly dim-witted pupil.

"Of course it is," he said. "But we're not going to go in by the front door, are we?"

"Of course not," said Shari. "That would be stupid, wouldn't it?"

Cruse nodded and cast a meaningful look in Kristas's direction.

"So how do we get there?" she asked.

"The same way I got here this morning," said Cruse and, in response to Shari and Kristas's look of confusion, pointed down to the ground.

He was standing over a metal grid.

Beneath the surface of Galileo lay an entire network of sewers, built when the first colonists had arrived on Pasiphae, and which had been designed to carry the waste from the terraformers' engineering projects far away from the main conurbations to dumping grounds.

The outlet from one of them led to ShantyLand. It had been bricked up years ago and left forgotten by the Board, who had feared that dissidents might use it to escape into the wilderness. Cruse had discovered it and over the years had opened it up again; it was from there that he had explored the whole of Pasiphae's capital city, undetected by the Galileans who lived and worked, unsuspecting, just a few metres above him.

The sewer network was almost a tiny city in itself, and, as they descended down a rusty and creaking ladder, Cruse warned them to be on the look-out for the retrogrades who, he said, inhabited these tunnels.

They were misfits and criminals who had been rejected even by the ShantyLanders; it was said that they were often so hungry that they weren't too proud to indulge in cannibalism. Viciously he told Shari that Doob might provide them with a tasty snack before they started on them.

Shari hugged Doob more closely to her, and exchanged an anxious look with Kristas. They had never suspected the existence of this subterranean series of passages before, or its flesh-eating inhabitants.

If knowledge of this had been hidden from them what else might the Board and the System have kept secret from their own citizens?

There was a mighty crash behind them, and they all turned to look. Unable to support Kili's weight, the rusty ladder leading down from the manhole into the sewers had pulled itself away from the wall. It had crashed down into the effluent and filth of the tunnel's floor.

Kili grunted apologetically and caught up with his human companions. Cruse just shook his head despairingly; he'd insisted that Kili be the last one to come down the ladder for precisely that reason.

"Crazy robot'll be the death of us all," he grunted as he tramped off down the darkened tunnel, the only light coming from the torch he carried in the pouch on his belt. The others hurried to keep up with him; if they lost him they might be trapped in the tunnels forever.

The next sixty minutes or so were some of the worst

of Shari's life. The sewers stank of methane and ammonia, making it difficult to breathe, and there were other sickly-sweet smells which made her want to vomit. It didn't help matters when Cruse cheerfully explained that they probably came from the decaying corpses of curious Galileans who had ventured down here and been killed by the sewer-dwellers.

The walls of the tunnels were covered in foul-looking mould and slime, and beneath their feet they couldn't help walking in the waste and rank effluents from the world above their heads. In the darkness they could also hear the threatening faraway cries of the cannibal inhabitants of the tunnels. Shari found herself walking closer and closer to Kili, as if he would offer her some protection from the nightmare she had thrown herself into. In her arms Doob pressed closer to Shari herself.

After about an hour's walking Cruse, who had remained silent for much of the journey, called them to a halt. He looked up at the ceiling above their heads. "This is as far as we go," he said.

"What do you mean?" asked Kristas, thinking the worst. "You're leaving us here?"

"I might have known it," Kili mumbled to himself. "Humans! Who can trust them..."

Cruse glared malevolently at them, and at Kili in particular, and pointed to a ladder almost hidden in the shadows on the wall; it led to a large iron grille set high in the roof.

"Where are we now?" asked Shari.

"Directly below the main runway of the space-port," he said.

"Won't there be armed guards there?" asked Kristas.

"Some," agreed Cruse. "Since travel restrictions have come into force the number of guards has increased, but they're not going to expect anyone to come from below ground. These sewers have been neglected and forgotten for years now."

He put a foot on the first rung of the ladder. "I'll go first, then you follow me, Shari, and then Kristas. The robot can take up the rear."

"The name is Kili," said Kili grumpily.

As Shari followed Cruse up the ladder she asked him: "Why are you doing this, Cruse? Putting your life in danger for people you hardly even know?"

Cruse continued climbing and didn't turn around to look at her. "The ten thousand credits," he said casually.

They're not going to be a lot of use to you if you end up dead, Shari thought, realizing that beneath his gruff and surly appearance there was a lot more to Cruse than met the eye.

Finally the top of the ladder was reached and, with some difficulty, Cruse managed to push open the metal grille and pulled his way to the surface. Doob hurried after him, grateful to be allowed out into the fresh air again, and was quickly followed by the others.

"Some escape route you chose for us," said Kristas as he tried to wipe the effluent and waste off his boots. "We're going to stink for weeks."

"There'll be even viler stinks once you get off Pasiphae," Cruse said with something approaching relish. "If you're already missing your starched sheets and freshly laundered clothes you know the way back." Kristas scowled at him.

"Where are we?" asked Shari, as she looked around her.

They had come out by the side of a roughly constructed building which appeared to be a hangar of some sort. The manhole was behind a stack of fuel drums which afforded them some cover. Beyond the hangar there stretched a wide tarmacked expanse, dotted here and there with all manner of small craft. Maintenance trucks drove speedily across the tarmacked surface, while on the outskirts of the landing strip, heavy tank-like vehicles cruised the area. On the perimeter of the field there were several tall lookout towers, which slowly swept the entire area with searchlights.

"Spaceport Five," said Cruse. "It's from here that all the short flights to Jupiter leave."

Shari looked around at the spacecraft parked on the tarmac, and was reminded of pictures she had seen of the tiny air-fields in the 20th century. All of the ships here were small and flimsy-looking too; few of them looked capable of a long-haul flight to TerraNova.

"Are you mad, Cruse?" she said. "TerraNova is millions of miles from us. You don't expect us to get there in one of those?"

"I'm no fool," he snarled, and looked nervously around. "Where's that blasted monkey of yours got to?"

As soon as she had climbed out of the manhole leading from the sewers, Doob had scampered off towards the hangar building. Terrified lest she be discovered, Shari ran after her.

"Shari! You blasted fool!" hissed Cruse, as the girl stepped out from the cover of the fuel drums in pursuit of Doob. The mercenary slipped out from his cover to try and grab Shari before she gave their presence away.

Luck seemed to be on their side as Cruse ran after the two: the engineers on the airfield were too concerned with their tasks to notice the three figures darting in the shadows.

Then Kili, concerned for Shari's safety, decided to help. Seven feet tall, he had been forced to crouch behind the fuel drums, but now he stood up to his full height – and accidently knocked over several drums which fell crashing to the ground.

A searchlight was instantly turned on the area by the guards manning the control towers. Kili and

Kristas stood transfixed, like two rabbits caught in the glare from the lights of an oncoming vehicle.

Another searchlight bathed Cruse and Shari in its brilliant white light. Doob, whom Shari had managed to catch up with, whimpered in her arms.

"Remain still, all of you," boomed a voice, as a security truck began to rumble across the field towards them.

Cruse glanced around him quickly, sizing up the situation. To their left about thirty metres away was the sleek black shape of a skimmer. The skimmer was about thirty metres long, with curved black fins, and a gun turret running the entire length of its top-hull. On its portside the airlock was open: obviously engineers had been working inside the craft, perhaps preparing it for take-off later in the day. The skimmer was a reconnaissance craft, intended for flying over the mining areas of Jupiter: Cruse realized it might be their only chance.

The security truck rumbled ever closer to Cruse and Shari; with a gulp Shari saw that the guards at the wheel were all armed. Cruse nodded over to the skimmer.

"When I say run, you run," he whispered from out of the corner of his mouth.

Shari looked nervously over at the skimmer and then back to Kili and Kristas who were also being approached by a security truck.

"But Kili and Kristas . . ." she began until Cruse cut her short.

"Forget about them," he said coldly.

The guards were almost upon them now. Cruse's hand went to the gun at his side, in a movement so slow and sure that only the most eagle-eyed of the guards would have noticed.

"You ready?" he asked.

Shari nodded.

"OK . . . now – *run!*"

As he barked out the order so he whipped out his gun from his side holster and fired directly at the front of the truck. As the explosive projectile from the weapon hit the windscreen it exploded in a shower of shattered glass. Another shot, and Cruse hit the engine, which erupted in a tower of flame and smoke.

The other guards who were approaching Kili and Kristas suddenly turned around and sped over to help their colleagues who were tumbling out of their damaged vehicle, dazed and shocked.

Shari's legs ached and her breath cut her throat like a rusty knife as she raced towards the open airlock door of the skimmer. Above Doob's screeches of terror and the blaring of alarm sirens, she was dimly aware of the rat-a-tat-tat sounds of gunfire. The guards had started firing on her and Cruse, who was racing after her towards the ship.

Not daring to turn around, she heard Cruse's

shouted curses, as he launched volley after volley of explosive projectiles at their attackers. She wondered how long it would be before he ran out of bullets: the skimmer, now only some five metres away, seemed impossibly distant.

Suddenly she heard a massive roar, and a whoop of triumph from Cruse. My God, he's actually enjoying this! she realized, as she put the first of her shaking feet onto the bottom rung of the ladder which led up to the airlock. Doob leapt out of her arms and shot, terrified, up into the ship.

Cruse had hit a fuel tank which had exploded in a plume of flame. Flames lashed out at neighbouring fuel tanks until a large part of the air-field was a sheer wall of fire. The disorientated guards veered their vehicles away from the conflagration, before rounding on their quarry once again.

Shari clambered up the ladder and flung herself into the skimmer. The cockpit was cramped, capable of holding no more than five or six people at the most, she guessed. Most of the skimmer's thirty-metre length was taken up by its powerful engines, she realized.

Cruse was fast on her heels and climbed into the cockpit, pushing rudely past her as he made his way to the bank of controls at the front of the craft. He had been hit by one of the guard's bullets and Shari winced at the sight of the ugly wound.

Quickly he scanned the controls. He seemed to

hesitate, as though this control panel was different in some ways from the ones he was familiar with. Then he selected one particular touch-sensitive control and the airlock door began to close.

"You can't leave!" screamed Shari. "What about Kili and Kristas!"

She pointed out of the cockpit window. Kili was carrying Kristas in his arms, and racing over the tarmac towards them. Projectiles burst harmlessly off the robot's parondite shell, as he cradled Kristas away from the line of fire.

Cruse grunted and reluctantly opened the door, just as Kili and Kristas reached the craft. As soon as they had clambered on board he slammed the door shut.

"Damn you, robot!" he cried, and then turned to Shari: "And damn your pet too!"

"You were going to leave without us!" accused Kristas, but Cruse wasn't listening. Instead his hands were flickering over the control panels of the skimmer, trying to coax the skimmer into action. Onboard navigational instruments began to tinkle into life, and as he operated another control the life-support systems came into operation, filling the cabin with a dull and soporific hum.

Shari pointed out through the view portals set above the control deck. Streams of guards were pouring out of adjoining buildings and running towards them. So far the skimmer seemed to be withstanding their gunfire but Shari had no idea how long that would last.

She grabbed Cruse's arm. "Get us out of here!" she cried.

Cruse looked in rapt attention at the LED display before him, while his hands flicked automatically over the controls. The floor beneath them began to vibrate as he engaged the engines, and the skimmer slowly began to move. Cruse adjusted the controls, preparing for take-off and the craft began to pick up speed.

Shari grabbed Kristas's hand: it looked like they were going to make it after all!

By their side Kili remained silent, carefully watching Cruse at the controls.

Suddenly the entire craft shuddered to a sickening halt. Shari and Kristas looked anxiously at each other and Cruse cursed again.

"What's happened?" she asked.

Cruse indicated the LED display; flashing on the screen were the words MISSION ABORTED. Outside the security guards were coming closer and closer.

"They've interfaced into the main flight computer," said Cruse. "They've stopped us dead by remote control."

"Can they do that?" asked Kristas in amazement.

"They just have," came the sardonic reply. "All these small reconnaissance craft are linked to one central computer."

"You should have taken one of the other craft then," Kristas reproved.

"I was going to," Cruse spat the words out, "until you and your metal friend there ruined it for us!"

Shari stepped between the two men. "Isn't there anything you can do?" she asked. Outside the skimmer was being surrounded by armed guards.

"We'd never be able to override the system in time," Cruse said angrily. "What we need is a computer more powerful than theirs to give us time to get away."

"Perhaps I may be able to assist."

Everyone turned to look at Kili.

"You?" asked Cruse in disbelief.

"Of course if you don't want my help, I can just sit back and watch you all get captured..."

Cruse stood up from the pilot's seat. "Be my guest, robot," he said sarcastically.

"Thank you."

Kili stood at the control board, studying and assessing the ship's capabilities, for a few brief seconds. Then he took out a lead from his chest unit which he plugged into a socket in the control board, interfacing with the central computer which controlled the skimmer.

A few seconds later he "unplugged" himself, and, armed with the information he had taken from the computer, he flashed his hands over the controls, flipping this switch and adjusting that meter. He moved so fast that his hands were just a blur. Finally he punched a hundred-digit number on the keyboard which lay to the left of the control panel. He turned to Cruse.

"I think you will find that I have improved our situation a little," he said, somewhat superciliously, thought Kristas.

"We're moving!" Shari cheered, and even Doob recognized the importance of the occasion and began to chitter cheerfully to herself.

Cruse gave Kili a slap on the back. "Thanks, robot," he said.

"I assure you it was nothing," came the smug reply. "Any *cybernetic* intelligence could have done it."

Cruse ignored the slight and began to steer the skimmer towards the guards who, as one, quickly ran out of its path. As the craft sped down the runway, gathering the necessary speed for take-off, the guards fired after it. The lights on the on-board computer winked crazily.

"What are they trying to do?" Shari shouted above the whooshing noise of increased speed.

"Trying to cut in on the computer again," said Cruse matter-of-factly, as he checked the various flashing displays beneath his finger-tips.

"But if they do that while we're travelling at this speed ..." Kristas's words died in his throat, as the entire craft began to shudder again.

"That's right," said Cruse, "we'll break up. Let's hope your metal friend got his calculations right!"

"But they can't just kill us," said Kristas. "Just because we want to leave."

"Just give them the chance!"

The noise of the engines was deafening now, as the skimmer gathered speed. On either side of them the buildings and hangars of Spaceport Five flashed by like a speeded-up vid-film.

Shari yelped with horror as she saw that they were approaching a steep ramp. Like a maniac, Cruse was steering them directly towards it and they were going to crash into it. She grabbed Kristas once more, shutting her eyes, preparing for the inevitable impact.

Instead she was flung to the floor, along with Doob and Kristas, as the skimmer climbed and shot off the ramp, launching itself up into the sky. She felt an enormous pressure on her chest as the G-forces rammed mercilessly into her, practically crushing her ribs and viciously squeezing the air out of her lungs.

She opened her eyes. The ship's cabin was spinning sickeningly around her. In the pilot seat Cruse was operating the controls as though nothing untoward was happening; there was an intense look of concentration on his face as he stared out into the dark sky of Pasiphae.

By her side Kristas lay unconscious and Doob, scarcely comprehending what was happening, was whimpering softly to herself.

Shari gasped, still finding it difficult to breathe. She tried to call out to Cruse but no words came from her mouth. She suddenly felt inexplicably sleepy.

Is this what dying is? she asked herself, as a dark cloud slowly descended upon her and the surrounding air became suddenly ice-cold.

Then everything went black, and Shari found merciful release from her ordeal.

One Week to Earth

The young creature on board the egg-shaped craft suddenly experienced a sharp intake of breath as it registered the presence of the moving blip on the scanner screen before it. Its blood-shot eyes opened wide in amazement and its huge nostrils flared in anticipation.

Cautiously it peered more closely at the screen, as if it didn't quite believe what it was seeing. There, amidst the stationary blips which represented Jupiter and its satellites, *something else* was moving.

Too small to be a space cruiser, this blip was moving in a haphazard and unpredictable pattern, as if it was trying to avoid detection by the most sophisticated tracking instruments of its home world. The Seti's instruments were far more precise and sensitive, the creature reflected smugly. For a race whose civilization was many thousands of years old, and which had learnt as much as the Seti had, tracking down one particular grain of sand in a desert the size of a planet was merely child's play. With their reliance not just on technology but on the psychic forces buried deep in the mind, the Seti had reached an understanding of the laws of Nature which the humans on TerraNova were just beginning to learn. Indeed, it could even be said that the Seti had some sort of command over almost all the natural laws and processes of the universe.

All, the creature sadly reflected, *except the most important one*. They were unable to prevent their own death, their own extinction.

Finally satisfied that the moving blip represented what it suspected, the creature instructed one of its attendant slaves to inform the other Seti on board the craft. The slave grunted obediently, and scampered off down the long winding corridors of the ship.

The young Seti turned back to the screen, and snorted with pleasure. Clouds of methane gas were emitted from its nostrils.

Everything was proceeding exactly as it should be, the Seti reflected, just as it had always been planned. Already the tiny ship represented on the screen was leaving the moon of Jupiter and heading towards the centre of the Solar System. Little did the people on board that ship realize the role they were now committed to play in the greatest mass extinction of a species the Universe had ever known.

The young Seti chuckled to itself: their agents on Pasiphae had performed their tasks well.

PART 2

The System

The Great Donovan Trueheart

The great Donovan Trueheart sat back in his leather easy-chair and sipped at his glass of wine, a vintage from the now-devastated vineyards back on Old Earth. He still liked to refer to mankind's original home by its former name rather than the new-fangled designation of the Home Planet: for one thing, it instilled in his followers a sense of history and belonging.

That sense of belonging was vital if he was to keep the iron hold on them he had had for the past fifteen years, ever since he had become the leader of the grouping known popularly as the EarthLifers.

The influence of the EarthLifers on System politics was immense, even though they were not, strictly speaking, a political party. Indeed, the System allowed for no political parties save the ruling one; but the EarthLifers' appeal to the general people was so strong that the President had recognized their power years ago and had appointed Trueheart head of System Security.

It was a role which he had cherished, one which had guaranteed him unlimited power and influence over almost every aspect of System life. Donovan Trueheart's spies were everywhere, checking up on anyone who might be considered a threat to the System and, by extension, Trueheart's own power base.

People lived in fear of the jack-booted sound of his security troops, as they patrolled areas of cities which Trueheart had suddenly deemed to be AUs, or Areas of Unrest; disgruntled children reported their parents when they spoke ill of the System, and old women on meagre pensions informed on their own neighbours, eager for the financial rewards that Trueheart's officials would bestow on them, and never once asked questions when those neighbours disappeared, never to be heard of again. It pleased Donovan Trueheart to see that everyone in the System had such a fine sense of social responsibility.

There was not a single leaf that could fall on TerraNova, people would say, or a kilogram of uranium mined on Neptune that Donovan Trueheart didn't know about. Indeed, Trueheart made it a matter of principle to know the darkest secrets of all his colleagues in Government. That way he had control over them.

For instance, he knew that the President wouldn't have tolerated his continual interference with her policies for so long if he hadn't known that ten years ago she had embezzled billions of credits from System funds for her own personal use. It was hardly surprising that he knew – after all, he had made sure that the credits were available for her to embezzle – but ever since then she had shown a healthy respect for him. In fact, Donovan Trueheart could have been regarded as System President in all but name; but he preferred to work behind the scenes, believing that the little people, as he called the inhabitants of the Twenty-One Worlds, distrusted ostentatious displays of power.

The video screen in its fine mahogany box by his side displayed the presumed flight path of the Seti ship as it approached TerraNova, or Mars as he liked to call it. The authorities had known about the Seti for many years past, and even now, when it was only a matter of days before they would intrude upon inhabited space, the System authorities still had not decided what was to be done with the aliens.

The System was made up of weak and spineless fools, thought Donovan Trueheart, as he remembered the prevarication shown by the System's President when she had been asked whether she considered the Seti to be hostile or not.

"We must all be patient and wait until contact has been made with them," she had said, not realizing that by that time it would be much too late.

In the opinion of Donovan Trueheart, leader of one of the greatest inspirational movements humanity had ever known, Man was the peak of perfection, indeed only one step removed from the angels themselves. It was a philosophy which had gained him countless thousands of followers both on Terra-Nova and on the colony worlds of Jupiter and Saturn, as well as billions of credits in his own personal bank account. People might fear him as head of System Security; as the spokesman for the glory of all humanity, they loved him in their millions.

Donovan Trueheart didn't care whether the intentions of the aliens were good or evil. The situation, as he saw it, was simple in the extreme: the Seti threw into doubt Mankind's role in the grand scheme of things, and, more specifically, his own position in that grand scheme. Therefore, the Seti must be blasted out of the skies before they came anywhere near to contaminating Earth and Mars with their filthy existence.

Donovan Trueheart took another long sip of his wine and burped appreciatively. Already in countless cities on TerraNova people were demonstrating against the arrival of the Seti, fomenting even more distrust and unease amongst the general populace.

Initial rumours, cunningly planted by Trueheart,

about the Seti's approach had given rise to a reluctant public admission by the President that the aliens were indeed on their way to the System. It had been a well-orchestrated protest movement, secretly designed by Trueheart to give the maximum exposure to his own views. Why, after the destruction of the Seti he might rise to a position of even higher importance than he held today. He stood up and looked vainly at his tall and slender figure in one of the full-length mirrors which lined the walls of his office.

Donovan Trueheart, Saviour of All Mankind. It had a nice ring to it, he decided, and if the title helped to fill his already overflowing coffers, well, then so much the better.

Quester

$\mathcal{S}$hari groaned as she felt something moist touch her brow. She struggled to open her eyes, and slowly her vision came into focus. Kristas was kneeling above her, mopping her face with a wet cloth. His brow was furrowed with concern.

"Are you all right?" he asked.

"I think so," she croaked, and tried to sit up. Kristas helped her, and even Doob scampered over to her side. "What happened?"

"The G-forces, as we escaped Pasiphae's gravity," came Cruse's voice from the far end of the cockpit. He chuckled evilly. "I suppose I should have warned you."

Shari glared at the mercenary in the pilot seat and

then stopped, as the import of his words hit her: *As we escaped Pasiphae's gravity?*

She looked expectantly at Kristas who nodded.

"We've made it?" she asked, scarcely able to believe him.

"Look outside, Shari," he said, and pointed to the vid-screens above the control deck which displayed the immediate environment outside the ship.

Shari gasped, as she took in the image on the screen. Jupiter and its satellites were now no more than rapidly receding dots seen in the vastness of space. From this distance it seemed hard to believe that millions upon millions of people were going about their lives, unaware of her and her friends' existence.

Beyond Jupiter, stars, their light no longer diffused by the artificial atmosphere of Pasiphae, blazed bright and steady. And beyond them, hidden in that deep and cold blackness was all that emptiness . . . *all that freedom. . . .*

Shari thought that now should be the time to cry. Instead she shuddered, as a feeling of new-found liberation coursed through her body. She looked down to find that Kristas was holding her hand in a comradely gesture of sympathy.

She turned away from the vid-screens, and looked at Cruse.

"That's what's outside the ship?" she asked, trying to come to terms with it.

Cruse sighed. "No, it's the in-flight entertainment, a vid-disk I'm running for your amusement," he said scornfully. "Of course it's what outside the blasted ship!"

"Then we've succeeded," said Kristas.

"We've left Jovian space," said Cruse. Kristas detected an unusual tone of uncertainty in Cruse's voice.

"Then we're on course for Mars?" he asked urgently.

Cruse shook his head. "Not yet."

Shari was suddenly afraid, remembering Kristas's earlier reservations about the mercenary. Cruse was a criminal: what did he have planned for them? "But you promised..."

Cruse turned round to look at her. "And believe it or not I keep my word," he growled. "But your blasted monkey means a big change in our plans."

Shari cradled Doob defensively in her arms. "What d'you mean?"

"This skimmer isn't my choice of craft," he said angrily. "But when Security spotted you chasing after your blasted pet I had to take the first craft I could reach."

He indicated the control panel in front of him. "This skimmer is used for travelling between Jupiter and its moons," he continued. "It isn't designed for interplanetary travel."

"You mean we can't get to Mars?" Shari asked apprehensively.

Cruse nodded. "Not without refuelling first of all," he said. "If we're lucky we have enough fuel cells to take us to one of the outer moons. There we'll commandeer another craft and travel to the Asteroid Belt and then on to Mars." He laughed. "With any luck we'll arrive there just as the Seti are knocking on the System's front door!"

"Then how long will it take?" asked Shari.

Cruse chuckled, and gestured around the small cabin. "In this ship I'd say about two months."

"*Two months!*"

Cruse grinned, revealing his yellow teeth. He opened the pouch at his side and took out a greyish protein bar which he chomped greedily on.

"That's right. I don't suppose you've brought any food with you?"

Shari and Kristas looked at each other, suddenly feeling very foolish.

"I thought not," said Cruse, and looked greedily at Doob who was clutched in Shari's arms. He licked his lips. "Well, I suppose we'll find something to eat..."

"There will be some food in the supply lockers," said Kili who had remained strangely silent up to now. He opened a small cupboard by the airlock door, and took out several packs of nutrient bars.

"Snacks," said Cruse dismissively. "They won't last us long enough," he added malevolently.

Kili turned to face the human. If Shari hadn't known better she would have said that the robot had taken an extreme dislike to the mercenary.

"Indeed not," he agreed. "Humans have a very inferior energy-producing mechanism. However, used sparingly, these supplies will be adequate for a three-day journey."

"Weren't you listening to me, robot?" asked Cruse. "If we get another ship this trip is going to take us two months; and that's only if we're lucky."

Kili walked over to the control deck. "I think not," he said confidently. "Spaceport security could easily have blasted us out of space – but they didn't."

"Perhaps they didn't want to kill us?" said Kristas, although he didn't believe it.

Kili clicked scornfully, and even Cruse by his side chuckled.

"The System is closed, and does not allow people to travel off-world without permission," Kili said matter-of-factly. "It is quite prepared to slaughter innocents to enforce its laws."

Shari frowned: Cruse had told them of the corrupt nature of the System's government, and she and Kristas had suspected it for a long time. This was the first time, however, that Kili had ever acknowledged it.

"We were, as you might by now have noticed, not

blasted out of existence," the robot continued. "Therefore we must search out the reason why."

Cruse regarded the robot with a new-found, albeit grudging, respect. The same thought had occurred to him too. He laughed to himself: here he was, worrying that he wasn't dead!

Kili indicated the control deck, and then turned back to Cruse, who avoided his gaze.

"This skimmer is not of standard System issue," Kili claimed.

Shari and Kristas looked hopelessly at each other: they couldn't tell one set of controls from another. Cruse, however, remained silent and stroked his chin thoughtfully, looking at the robot through narrow, untrusting eyes. He realized that Kili knew he wasn't completely familiar with the layout of this particular control deck, but he was damned if he was going to reveal that information to Shari and Kristas.

"Indeed it makes use of sub-tachyon technology," Kili concluded, as though that explained everything.

Shari and Kristas shrugged at each other, but Cruse's face suddenly lit up as he turned back to the controls and flitted his eyes over them.

"Good God, the robot's right!" he said.

"I usually am," was the predictable reply.

"Sub-tachyon technology?" asked Kristas. By his side, Shari frowned: the words seemed oddly familiar to her. She closed her eyes, trying to remember the last time she had heard the words spoken: the words came back to her in her father's voice.

"A tachyon is supposed to be an atomic particle, which can travel faster than the speed of light," said Cruse, as if that explained everything.

"Supposed to be?"

"Their existence has not yet been conclusively proven," Kili offered.

"And this ship makes use of tachyon technology?" asked Shari.

"No. *Sub*-tachyon technology. That is what I have said, Shari," said Kili. "It enables us to travel at a fraction of the speed of light. But to be able to travel at even one-tenth of the speed of light is an impressive achievement."

"But why's it called sub-tachyon technology?" asked Kristas.

"If tachyon technology did exist," said Cruse, "then that would mean that we could travel faster than the speed of light."

"And that is, of course, impossible," said Kili, sounding just as if he was delivering a lecture to a group of eager students. "Sub-tachyon technology is the closest mankind will ever get – for the moment."

"That doesn't stop the System working on it," said Cruse, "I've heard rumours of some big project."

"Rumours do not concern me, Mr Cruse," Kili suddenly said. "I am a Mark Seven ServoRobot and I deal in facts." He sighed. "And the strangest things could happen if humans started messing around with the speed of light."

Kristas held up his hands to silence the mercenary and the robot. "But what's all this got to do with us not being attacked by security?"

"Security wouldn't dare to blow us up," said Cruse. "The on-board technology's too valuable to them."

"Precisely," said Kili. "And by using the skimmer's sub-tachyon drive we should be able to reach TerraNova within three days – long before your food supplies run out."

Shari and Kristas beamed, and let out a whoop of triumph. Even Cruse couldn't suppress a grin, before turning to Kili again.

"I'll say one thing for you, robot, you know a lot about the latest technology for someone who's just a ServoRobot."

"I am a most voracious reader, sir," Kili replied. "I have interfaced with many computer data bases in my time."

"I'm sure you have," Cruse said knowingly, and turned his attention back to the controls.

Cruse was a skilled engineer and now that he knew the function of the unfamiliar controls he was able to assess their use and applications, with a little help from Kili. He began to make adjustments to the controls, engaging the skimmer's sub-tachyon engines. He grimaced as another LED flashed up before him, and he raised his hands in desperation.

"What's wrong?" asked Kristas.

"The blasted on-board computer needs a numerical ID," he said. "Until I give it the correct code I won't be able to operate the engines."

All three of them looked hopefully at Kili.

"Well?" demanded Cruse through gritted teeth. "You seem to have all the answers, robot."

Kili paced about the cabin, clearly relishing all the attention which was being shown to him. Finally he yawned theatrically (Robots don't yawn, Kili! Shari thought angrily. Get to the point!)

"Well, if you want my guess, I would suggest 240758 2011 59743 8000.261 05777 17504," he said casually. "Of course, that is only a wild guess."

Cruse had already punched in the figures on the flight-deck keyboard. The cabin was filled with the sound of the sub-tachyon engines engaging themselves. Cruse glanced up triumphantly at Kili.

"Well done, robot," he said, before returning to the deck where his hands flicked speedily over the controls.

"Merely a lucky guess," Kili said smugly.

"C'mon, Kili," said Shari, not taken in for a minute. "How did you know?"

"The engagement codes were in the Security computer," explained Kili. "When I interfaced with it

I picked up those codes as well. It was a simple enough procedure – for a *robot*, that is."

"Thanks anyway, Kili," said Kristas. "Not only are we going to reach Mars before we run out of food, but we're also going to be safe from any security ships out to track us down."

"How do you come to that asinine conclusion?" asked Cruse.

"If this sub-tachyon technology is so new," said Kristas, with a superior air, "then few security ships are going to be able to catch up with us."

Cruse looked at Kili.

"He's got a point," he said. "That is, if this sub-tachyon technology is as rare and underdeveloped as you say it is."

"Of course it is," said Kili.

Shari stepped in between the two enemies. "We've all been lucky so far," she said.

Cruse ignored her, and continued to stare at Kili. "Yes, we have, haven't we?" he said meaningfully. "Very lucky indeed..."

He turned his attention once more to the controls. The cabin shuddered again as the sub-tachyon engines took over and the skimmer shot through space to its destination of TerraNova.

Travelling at almost a hundredth the speed of light the skimmer would have appeared as nothing more than a gleaming blur to the tracking instruments of the System government.

But, unknown to Shari and her friends, there were other instruments monitoring the skimmer's progress to TerraNova. These instruments could detect the heartbeats of Shari, Cruse, Kristas and Doob, and even the cybernetic pulses of Kili; they could detect every single iota of sub-tachyon energy being used by the skimmer, and predict to the nanosecond the moment when the skimmer would approach Terra-Novan space.

These were instruments of a technology thousands of years ahead of Mankind's, a technology which had long ago mastered the sub-tachyon technology that Mankind was only now discovering. There were instruments scarcely dreamed of by Mankind's philosophers and artificers, instruments which had been in operation for hundreds of years now, waiting for this one particular moment.

The plans of the Seti were finally coming to fruition.

Twenty-four hours passed on the skimmer. Cruse had been at the controls for almost all that time, pausing only for a three-hour rest when he had reluctantly handed over the controls of the skimmer to Kili. Shari marvelled at his determination, and wondered just why he was helping them so much. She had noticed a curious gleam in his eyes, the look not of a mercenary on the make, but of a pioneer.

Cruse spent little time talking to her and Kristas,

apparently regarding them as little more than human baggage. So why is he doing all this for us? she asked herself. It can't just be for the money surely?

She nibbled at a piece of protein wafer. Already her stomach was rumbling but Cruse had imposed a strict rationing on their food supplies.

When Kristas had attempted to take more than his fair share, Cruse had rounded on him, and waved his gun menacingly in his face. Surprisingly Kili had backed Cruse up.

After that the atmosphere on board the skimmer had been so tense that they could have cut it with a knife.

Cruse briefly glanced round to look at Shari and Kristas, and then flicked several switches on the control panel before him. The cabin of the skimmer shuddered once more. Kristas stood up and strode over to the control deck.

"What are you doing?" he demanded.

"Switching off the tachyon engines," said Cruse. "And re-engaging normal power. If we entered planetary atmosphere at sub-tachyon speed we'd break up."

He nodded to the vid-screen directly in front of them: they were rapidly approaching a small rocky planetoid.

Kristas frowned. "That's not Mars ...'" he said. Shari, who had joined them by the control deck, felt a shiver of apprehension run down her spine.

"No, it's not," Cruse said, refusing to divulge any further information.

"We had a deal!" said Shari. "Where are you taking us?"

Cruse smirked, but still said nothing. He continued to operate the controls.

Shari turned despairingly to Kili. It was clear that their doubts about Cruse had been correct; now she feared the worst.

"The object we are now approaching is called Avernus," he volunteered.

Shari and Kristas exchanged blank looks, while Cruse chuckled silently to himself.

"It is an asteroid approximately halfway between Jupiter and TerraNova," the robot continued to explain. "It is also far enough off the main spaceways for it to be inhabited by criminals and pirates."

"You can't take us there!" said Shari. "Among all those criminals!"

"Why not?" laughed Cruse. "That's what you are now!"

Kristas grabbed Cruse by the shoulders. "You must take us to Mars!"

Cruse roughly pushed the younger man off him.

"Look, as far as I'm concerned you're a couple of rich kids off on a spree for kicks," he said. "I said I'd take you to Mars and I will. But you're not going to breach Mars security without one of these."

He activated a control and a small transparent card

popped out of a slit in the control deck. It was inlaid with micro-circuitry which glittered silver and gold in the light of the skimmer. He waved it in front of Kristas's face.

"Do you know what this is?" Kristas shook his head. "It's a transponder code, the identification code of our ship. Without one we'd never be able to get through Martian security."

"So?"

"We're a marked vehicle now," Cruse continued. "As soon as we reach Martian space they'll be able to track us down. So we're going down to Avernus first, to get a counterfeit one made for us."

"Ah ..." Kristas said and glanced sheepishly over at Shari.

"So why don't you learn to trust me, and do what I say?" Cruse said sourly. "That way we might just all of us get through this crazy little escapade alive!"

"I'm sorry, Cruse," said Shari. "You're right after all."

"I'm sorry too," said Kristas, although through gritted teeth.

Cruse gruffly acknowledged their apologies, and turned back to the controls.

Avernus was now looming large on the vid-screen. They would be there within the hour.

Avernus was a large asteroid so far away from the normal spaceways that many criminals and refugees from the System had made it their home. Murderers and thieves lived here, alongside the space pirates who plundered the asteroids for their valuable minerals, and escaped political prisoners. In many ways it was a larger version of ShantyLand, and Cruse seemed as much at home here as he had on Pasiphae.

Cruse had managed to land on a small plain overlooking the main settlement on the planetoid, and had wanted to go down to collect a transponder code by himself. Shari, however, had insisted that she accompany him: she was beginning to trust the rough and mean-mannered man more than before but still thought it wise to keep a wary eye on him.

As they walked through the narrow alleyways of the settlement Shari asked Cruse why he was helping them. Cruse shrugged.

"You gave me ten thousand credits," he said awkwardly. "Isn't that reason enough?"

"I don't think so," she said. "I saw that look in your eyes when we took off from Spaceport. You're doing this for something more than just money."

"Maybe I am," he said curtly. "But it's nothing you need to know about."

"If you'd only tell me—"

Cruse cut her short, and indicated a small brick hut at the end of an alleyway.

"This is where we're expected," he said, and ushered her into the tiny building.

Inside there was a small room, empty except for a

small table in the centre of the floor. The room was in darkness; Shari shivered. From somewhere in the shadows she could hear someone breathing.

Cruse seemed unperturbed. "Are you here?" he whispered. "It's me – Cruse..."

A tall figure shuffled out of the shadows, leaning on a walking cane for support. He was dressed in rags and tatters and his entire face was covered with a mask, behind which Shari could see his eyes burning with an intense ferocity.

"Welcome, Cruse – and welcome to your friend as well."

The old man's voice was weak and croaky, but there was something familiar about it too, Shari realized. She tried hard to remember where she had heard the voice before.

Cruse nodded a perfunctory greeting and then remarked on the old man's mask. He sighed.

"An accident, I fear," he said, all the time not looking at Cruse but at Shari. "The technology involved in forging a transponder code is hazardous," he continued. "The wounds will heal in time, though."

"Do you have what we want?" Cruse asked.

He nodded and took a small micro-chip out of his pocket and handed it over to him.

"This transponder code will identify you as a System-friendly ship," he said. "It won't get you into

Island Space however – you're on your own from thereon."

Island Space? Shari had never heard the words before and she looked to Cruse for the explanation that never came.

Cruse pocketed the transponder code, and nodded his thanks to the old man. "Thanks Que—"

The old man raised a finger to Cruse's lips, and looked meaningfully over at Shari. "I would prefer it if you didn't use my real name, Cruse ..." he said.

Cruse nodded curtly. "Thanks all the same."

"It's the least I can do," the old man said. "After all you've done for me."

And with that he turned and vanished once more into the shadows of his hut. Cruse and Shari left.

"What did he mean, 'after all you've done for me'?" Shari demanded, as they made their way back up to the plain and the skimmer.

"You don't let up, do you?" asked Cruse, and chuckled. "I helped to get some friends of his off-world once."

"For the money of course?" Shari smiled.

"Of course," said Cruse, and Shari didn't believe him in the slightest.

As they walked away from the tiny hut they heard the old man's voice shout after them.

"You'd better hurry along, Cruse – we're due for a storm tonight."

Cruse raised his eyes heavenwards: "Wonderful – that's all we blasted well need!"

"A storm?" asked Shari, and looked up at the sky too. Avernus had a breathable atmosphere of sorts, like many of the small moons and asteroids terraformed by mankind; but there was no trace of any storm in the cloudless sky. "What does he mean?"

"You'll see, Shari," said Cruse grimly, "you'll see..."

As soon as Cruse and Shari had left the old man started to chuckle to himself. He took off his mask to reveal a wizened face, lined with years, but unblemished by the wounds he claimed he had sustained in forging the transponder code.

The mask had been uncomfortable to wear, he reflected, but it had been necessary. It had been many years since Shari had seen him, but it would not have done if she had recognized him now as the man who had visited her father in his study on the last night that Shari had seen him alive.

It had been more recently that Kristas had seen him, when, as a member of the Board, he vetoed his travelling off-world. Quester was pleased that Kristas had shown the spirit he knew was in him. The young boy would still achieve his dream; but this way, as a rebel and a runaway from the System, he would also fit in with Quester's own plan.

He chuckled as he imagined what Kristas or Shari

would have said if they had recognized him. They would probably have wondered how he could be on Avernus ahead of them when he left sometime after they had departed from Pasiphae. That just proved that his disguise had been a wise move: it wouldn't have done to let them know that he had access to a technology superior to the sub-tachyon engines which drove their skimmer, a technology which he estimated wouldn't be invented in this region of space for another four hundred years or so.

The man known as Quester walked out of his hut and stared searchingly at the night sky. The technology which had brought him to Avernus before Shari's party had been left to him by the Seti. Soon they would be here in person – and years of patient waiting would finally come to fruition!

The skimmer rose effortlessly off the surface of Avernus and once more eased itself up into the blackness of interplanetary space. Because Avernus was much smaller than Pasiphae, its escape velocity was correspondingly lower, and neither Shari nor Kristas experienced the crippling G-forces they had succumbed to on their first trip off-world.

Shari and Kristas grinned at each other, feeling now like experienced space travellers. With the new transponder code installed in the ship's communication systems, they said, it seemed that the rest of the flight to TerraNova would be an easy one. In the pilot's seat Cruse burst out laughing.

"Don't you believe it," he said, as he fine-tuned the navigational controls. "We might be safe from System security at the moment but there's always the pirates."

"Pirates?" asked Kristas urgently.

"That's right," the older man replied.

"But why doesn't the System do something about them?"

"Why should it?" asked Cruse. "They're a minor irritant. They've learnt the law of survival just as we ShantyLanders did. As long as they don't strike at the heart of the System, as long as they don't stir up trouble amongst the people and get them to ask too many questions then they're left well alone. The System's like a wild and hungry wolf looking for its next meal: it's not going to worry about a few fleas. They cruise this sector of space plundering the asteroids for their minerals. I imagine they'd like to get their hands on a tachyon-powered skimmer as well..."

"But you'll be able to outmanoeuvre them in this, won't you?" Shari asked hopefully.

"Maybe," he answered, enjoying her disconcertedness. "And then maybe not."

Well, thanks for inspiring confidence in us then! thought Shari.

"Anyway that's the least of our worries," he said, and pointed at the vid-screen.

Ahead of them in the blackness they could see what appeared to be a cluster of gleaming dust specks, dancing like motes in a sunbeam. They must have been several kilometres away from them, but they were rapidly approaching them.

"Meteoroid storm," said Cruse, as casually as he might be announcing an approaching shower back in Galileo. "Five thousand tons of rock and metal. And we're heading straight for it."

"Then take us away from it!" urged Kristas, the panic rising in his voice.

Cruse shook his head.

"It'd take us too far out of our flight course," he said coolly, although Shari noticed that his knuckles were white as he pulled down on some of the navigational levers.

"Our best chance is to ride it out and try to avoid the big ones ..." He glanced up at the LED which displayed their course and speed. "Now hold on!" he cried, and rammed down hard on a control.

The skimmer sped off, heading straight for the heart of the storm.

The first meteoroid struck the skimmer with a bone-jarring and stomach-turning force.

Shari and Kristas were thudded to the floor of the cabin, while Doob whimpered in a corner, scarcely comprehending what was happening. Only the imperturbable Kili stood upright, watching Cruse steer the skimmer away from the larger rocks in the storm.

Cruse laughed, as he weaved in and out of the meteoroids, dodging the larger chunks of rock and metal, and hoping that the skimmer's hull would withstand the pounding given it by the smaller meteoroids in the storm.

He's enjoying this, Shari realized once more. It's like a huge game to him!

Cruse veered away from a huge ball of molten rock that was heading straight for the skimmer. As he did so another smaller boulder rammed straight into the side of the craft, shaking the occupants of the skimmer like dice in a can.

For a terrifying moment everything went black as the interior lighting of the ship automatically cut itself off. When the lights returned Cruse was lying motionless on the floor, having been thrown out of his seat by the shock of the impact. A trickle of blood was running down his temple.

Shari rushed to his side, trying to shake him back into consciousness. With Cruse out of action there was no way that they would be able to survive the meteoroid storm.

Another rock hit them, and then another and then another. The sound of their impact pounded remorselessly in their ears, deafening them. The floor shook and heaved underneath their feet, throwing Shari off-balance and away from Cruse.

Kristas scrambled over to her, while Doob screeched in terror. Along one wall a bank of instruments burst into flames; the cabin was suddenly filled with the acrid stink of escaping mercury vapour. The lights in the cabin began to flicker on and off again.

"Cruse!" Shari groaned, as she crawled back to the mercenary's side. "We must help Cruse."

Seemingly unconcerned by all the chaos around him Kili walked steadily over to the control deck. He looked briefly down at the flashing warning lights on the navigational panel, immediately assessing the situation.

"Tend to Mr Cruse, Shari," he said, his voice (for once) betraying no emotion whatsoever. "I will attend to the piloting of this ship."

Shari looked at Kili in amazement and then shrugged. She took a cloth from Cruse's pouch and began to dab at the blood on his temple. The injury was merely a flesh wound and the mercenary was already returning to consciousness.

At the control deck Kili adjusted the navigational instruments with a speed and a lightness of touch totally belied by his heavy seven-foot metal frame.

Immediately the pummelling from the meteoroids slackened, as the robot successfully guided the ship through the worst of the storm, his computer brain calculating the least dangerous route to take.

At the same time he shut down the instruments which had burst into flame, thereby ensuring that the flames and the escaped mercury vapour wouldn't spread.

He turned wearily to Kristas. "The fire extinguishers might be of some help now, don't you think?" he asked sarcastically.

Kristas got up off the floor and sheepishly began attending to the flames from the damaged control panels. Kili meanwhile continued to steer their course through the meteoroid storm.

By now Cruse was fully conscious and he shrugged away Shari's attentions and staggered to his feet. He stumbled over to Kili at the control deck.

"I'll take over now, robot," he growled.

"You have been injured," Kili stated flatly.

"I'll live," he said, and glared at the robot.

It was clear that Kili had no intention of leaving the control deck; and there was very little even Cruse could do to move two and a half tons of metal when it refused to budge.

"I must insist that Shari's life is not put into jeopardy," Kili continued. "And therefore I shall pilot the skimmer until you have returned to full strength."

"I said I'll take over now, robot," Cruse repeated, and then looked at Kili through narrowed suspicious eyes. "And besides you're a Mark Seven Servo-Robot...."

"That is correct."

"Mark Sevens aren't programmed for spaceflight," Cruse pointed out. "You're not *supposed* to know how to pilot this ship."

Kili was suddenly aware that all eyes were on him.

"Ah yes," he clicked. "That is something which I seem to have overlooked." He stood aside. "In which case, Mr Cruse, I hand over the running of the ship to you."

"Thank you," Cruse said sarcastically and sat down in the pilot's seat. The skimmer had almost left the meteoroid storm now, and they were sailing into clear space.

"There is one thing that you can do for me though," he said.

"I am always glad to be of service."

"You can go outside," Cruse continued. "I want to know how badly damaged the hull is."

Kili nodded his assent and proceeded to the airlock door. As soon as the door had shut behind him Cruse turned to Shari and Kristas.

"I don't trust the robot," he said flatly.

"Kili?" asked Shari in disbelief. "But he's my friend."

"He knows more than he's supposed to," Cruse said. "Where does he come from?"

"He's just a normal Mark Seven," said Shari. "He's

always been with my family; he helped to bring up my father and his father before him—"

"Well, I don't like him!"

Kristas walked up to Cruse. "Maybe we've just got a case of wounded egos here," he said.

"What d'you mean?" asked Shari.

"Kili got us safely out of Spaceport," Kristas reminded her, and then looked accusingly at Cruse. "He got us through the meteoroid storm alive when you were out cold on the floor. Perhaps it's Kili who should be the leader of this trip."

Cruse refused to let more than a brief flicker of anger show in his darkened eyes. "I don't trust robots," he said. "You know where you are with people. Human beings share a common culture and history; and even when they're double-dealing you, their body language always gives them away. With robots you never know what they're thinking or plotting. I found that out the hard way when they gunned down Marla and the others all those years ago. They're as inscrutable as these damn Seti you seem so interested in seeing. And just as dangerous."

"You're scared of the Seti?" accused Kristas. Even Kristas found it difficult to believe that this rough and spacewise mercenary could be frightened of anything or anyone.

Cruse sneered. "I'd be a fool not to be," he admitted. "We don't know what they are, why they're coming here. We don't even know what they look like. If they've the technology to cross inter-stellar space then they're thousands of years more advanced than us. Who's to say that they won't treat us as little more than laboratory animals waiting to be experimented on?"

"But if the Seti are so intelligent then they must know that that sort of behaviour is wrong ..." Shari's voice trailed away: suddenly she wasn't so sure.

"The truth is we don't know," Cruse said. "And we won't start to find any answers until we get to meet them. Until then we know as much about them as what goes on in that devious computer that robot of yours has the nerve to call a mind!"

Outside the skimmer, floating in space, Kili couldn't hear Cruse, but guessed what was going on. After all, he realized, once you accepted that human beings were probably one of the most illogical species in creation, then Cruse's feelings towards the creature who had just saved him was entirely predictable.

He adjusted his visual instrumentation to examine more closely the hull of the skimmer. There was only a little superficial damage, as he (and Cruse) knew there would be, and the skimmer would easily survive the journey to TerraNova. And after that he was sure that Cruse could find them transportation to take them on further to the Old Earth.

Kili turned his head away from the hull of the spacecraft and towards two shining points of light, sparkling millions of miles off in the distance of space. He adjusted his telescopic circuits to examine the objects more closely.

They were both planets, separated from each other by a little over fifty million miles. The closer one was TerraNova – the old Mars – only two days' flying time away from them now.

Beyond Mars there was the Home Planet, the Old Earth. It shone a greenish-red, the colour of rusty iron. Kili remembered the times when it was Mars that had been called the Red Planet; now the destruction and ruin on Earth was turning that once fertile world into a red planet, while the terraformed Mars bloomed green and blue in the darkness of space.

Kili sometimes wished he had been programmed with emotions: now felt like just the right time to sigh. He sighed anyway, and turned back to enter the airlock door.

As he did so, he noticed a purple-ish streak of light moving parallel to the skimmer. It must have been several million miles away but even from this distance Kili guessed that its flight path would eventually converge with that of the skimmer. That mysterious streak of light was immensely important not only to him but to the future of the entire human race, he knew.

When he returned into the ship through the airlock door Cruse, Shari, Kristas and Doob were waiting for him.

"Well, robot? Any damage?" asked Cruse.

"None at all," said Kili and then added: "You know, if you had wanted to talk behind my back you could have just asked me to switch my audio circuits off. There was no need to send me outside!"

Shari cringed with embarrassment, but behind her Cruse just laughed. He might be just a robot, he realized, but he shows a lot more sense than his two human companions put together!

"Kili, we didn't mean to . . ." Shari began, until Kili raised a hand to silence her.

"It's quite all right," he said. "I'm just a robot after all – *I* don't have feelings. . ."

"So what was it like out there, Kili?" Kristas interrupted quickly. Kili might not be supposed to have any feelings; but Kristas also knew that the robot could sulk with the best of them. "Did you see anything interesting?"

"Nothing, Kristas," replied Kili. "I saw nothing of any interest at all."

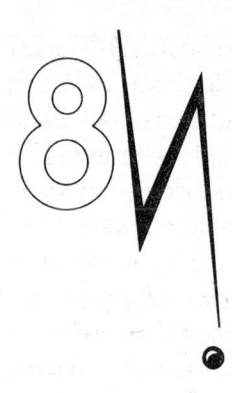

TerraNova

"It's beautiful," gasped Shari as she gazed down on one of the many tree-lined boulevards of New Canberra, the main city of TerraNova. "All that space..."

They were standing on the roof of one of the city's towering buildings, and far beneath them the citizens of TerraNova went about their business, unaware of the renegades' existence. The fake transponder codes had brought them safely past the planet's defence and security shields, and now it was time to marvel at the freedom enjoyed by other more fortunate members of the System.

Above them the two suns of Mars beamed down on them. One was the real sun, about 140 million miles away, the same yellow sun that had once warmed the cities and fields of Earth. Of course, it was much too far away to provide much warmth for the newly terraformed planet, so a second, artificial sun hung in the sky, a huge ball of carefully controlled nuclear and thermal energy constructed by the artificers of the terraforming programme.

In the distance a silvery-blue river snaked its way through the patches of green which covered the foothills of Olympus Mons, one of the largest mountains on the planet. Shari found it hard to believe that only a few hundred years ago this entire planet had been a bare and lifeless lump of rock; now it had become mankind's new adopted home.

It was in the foothills of Olympus Mons that Cruse had landed the skimmer, and it was there that Kili and Doob were waiting for them. Shari and Kristas, however, had insisted that they be taken to see New Canberra first. They had come so far that they thought they deserved to see the capital city, which many called one of the wonders of the System. Cruse had called them naive and sentimental, and said that they would probably get caught by System officials. They had insisted, and he had finally begrudgingly agreed, but not before he had conducted a brief foray into the city market where he had stolen olive-green tunics for them all to wear. That seemed to be the standard dress in New Canberra and he hoped that, so disguised, they would attract as little attention as possible.

"It's beautiful." Kristas echoed Shari's words.

"It still stinks," said Cruse dismissively.

Kristas looked evilly at him. "It's better than Pasiphae," he said.

"That's not difficult," Cruse sniggered. "Oh, TerraNova's bigger and prettier no doubt, so you think it's better. It's still run by the System; everything you do is still for the System, and dissent is crushed just as forcefully as it is back on Pasiphae."

"Why do you always look on the bad side?" Kristas asked.

"Because I'm usually right," came the instant reply. He looked at his two fellow travellers. "I've brought you here – what do you do now?"

Shari and Kristas looked at each other. The possibility of actually reaching TerraNova had seemed so unattainable that they had never paused to consider what they would do now that they had reached their destination.

"We will find my father," said Shari firmly.

"Oh will we now?" chuckled Cruse. "And have you any idea of where to start looking? This is a big planet, you know!"

"I don't care – I'll find him, somehow ..." she added feebly.

Cruse turned to Kristas. "And you, dreamer? Do you still want to meet the Seti?"

"Yes," he said adamantly. "And you promised to help us."

"Your father isn't going to be on TerraNova anyway," said Cruse.

Shari's face fell. "Then where . . . ?"

"He's a physicist," Cruse continued. "He'll be on one of the Islands."

Shari looked blank. She remembered the words the mysterious old man had used back on Avernus: *The transponder won't get you into Island Space however – you're on your own from thereon.*

"The Islands?"

"You won't find a scientist in New Canberra for love nor money these days," he explained. "The coming of the Seti has shaken up the world of science like nothing since . . . well, since Darwin's theory of evolution."

"So?" asked Kristas.

"They're all off-world," he said.

"They've gone to Earth?" he asked.

Cruse shook his head. "Can you see a bunch of well-to-do scientists surviving on that hell-pit of a planet for a day, let alone a few months? They'll be on one of the space stations in orbit between here and Earth."

"They're the Islands?" asked Shari. "Why haven't we heard of them?"

"Why hadn't you heard of the Seti until a short while ago?" he asked rhetorically. "Why weren't you allowed off-world? System believes that the common people are happier not knowing about the top-secret research establishments and the luxury living spaces enjoyed by its elite." He chuckled ironically. "Why, if they found out they might even become jealous – and that would never do now, would it?"

"Is the System really that corrupt?" asked Kristas, although by now he had already guessed the answer.

"To the core," said Cruse with feeling. "If you're content to function as its workers and slaves then you have no complaints. But start to ask questions, start to think for yourself, and then—" He made a croaking sound and drew his finger across his throat.

"So how do we get to these Islands?" asked Shari. "Will the skimmer be able to take us there?"

Cruse shook his head.

"By now the transponder code we used to breach Martian security will have been identified as a fake," he said. "We won't be able to use the same escape route again."

"So what do we do?"

Cruse considered Shari carefully. "Aren't you sure that you don't want to stay here on TerraNova?" he asked slyly. "I have friends here who could fix you up with a false set of papers."

He indicated the boulevards and parks stretched out beneath them. "It's a big world out there, Shari – there's a fifty-fifty chance that you'd never be tracked down by the authorities – and you'd have a freedom of sorts."

"I want to see my father," Shari declared firmly.

"And if TerraNova is anything like you say it is, then it's not going to be much better than Pasiphae, is it? I don't want to stay here."

Cruse looked at Kristas. "And what about you, dreamer?"

"I've come this far," the younger man said. "And I'm going even further."

Cruse nodded to himself, and regarded his younger companions with something approaching respect.

They were both a couple of idealistic fools, he decided, but they had spirit, there was no doubt of that. And what the hell, thought Cruse; there was a time when he too had been a young idealistic fool! He remembered Marla; he wondered what she'd say if she could have seen the hardened unfeeling mercenary he'd allowed himself to become.

He clapped his hands together in a decisive gesture. "Then I'll have to try and arrange some sort of transport to the Islands," he said and shook his head.

"Can you do it?" asked Kristas.

Cruse gave him a withering look. "As I said, I have friends here who help me ferry people to Earth—"

" 'That hell-pit of a planet', you called it," Kristas reminded him.

Cruse ignored the remark. "They might be able to help me smuggle you on board one of the Islands."

He turned to go, but Shari held him back.

"What do we do?" she asked.

Cruse laughed. "What every tourist does when

they arrive on a new planet!" he said. "Go and see the sights!"

New Canberra was the political, financial and cultural centre of the entire System. What New York had been in the 20th century, Tokyo in the 21st, and Beijing in the 22nd, so New Canberra was today.

Every morning thousands upon thousands of people poured down its tree-lined boulevards, on their way to work, content and secure in the knowledge that they were living in the most cosmopolitan, efficient and cultured city in the whole twenty-one inhabited planets of the System. They, of course, conveniently forgot about the rumours of riots on the outskirts of the city, in protest of the coming of the Seti. After all, the riots had not been reported by the World News Network, so they couldn't have happened, could they?

In such a vast and crowded metropolis Shari and Kristas passed virtually unnoticed in their olive-green suits as they sauntered along the walkways, admiring the functional yet pleasant architecture, and relaxing in the small squares and parks which dotted the city.

Yet, for all its formal beauty, there was something about it which disturbed Shari and Kristas. It wasn't the giant posters which seemed to adorn every street corner featuring the face of the President or Donovan Trueheart, or urging the people to work even harder, or extolling the virtues of "One People, One President, One System". It was Kristas who finally identified what was wrong with the System's capital.

"It's got no *soul*, Shari," he said. "The buildings, they're all so perfect, so stylized..."

"I know what you mean," she said, remembering the time she had visited St Paul's Cathedral and the Taj Mahal in the Virtual Reality room. The architects and builders of those two monuments had put their whole life and love in their work. The buildings of New Canberra, on the other hand, might as well have been designed by the uncaring and unfeeling hand of a computer, as indeed they had been.

This absence of emotion showed, too, in the people walking along the crowded streets in their drab olive-green uniforms. Their eyes seemed blank, fixed only on their task in hand, and their faces were lacking any expression. Serving the System was their life: they were not paid to stand and stare. Suddenly even ShantyLand seemed bizarrely attractive to Shari and Kristas.

"How can people live like this?" Shari asked.

"We did once," said Kristas.

Pasiphae and the Academy now seemed unimaginable years away. Their decision to leave, and their flight into space had changed both of them much more than they had realized.

Kristas tried to change the subject. "What do we do now?" he asked. "We've still hours to go before we meet up with Cruse."

Shari beamed. "There's one place I've always wanted to go to on TerraNova," she said. "Ever since I was a little girl, in fact."

Kristas groaned good-naturedly; he should have known what was coming. "And where might that be, Shari?" he asked even though he knew what her answer was going to be.

"The dinosaurs!" Shari said. "Let's go and visit the dinosaurs!"

When Earth had been evacuated all those hundreds of years ago, the collections of most of the planet's museums had been destroyed or left behind to rot. A Michelangelo sculpture or a Van Gogh painting would hardly prove to be of any use as mankind attempted to build a new life on Mars, the System had argued.

The only exceptions were the contents of the major science museums around the planet. These had been carefully packed and labelled and transported out to the new museum complex in New Canberra, where they were exhibited and presented as evidence of humanity's superiority over all other forms of nature.

And of all the displays in the complex the most popular, beyond any doubt, was the dinosaur hall. Even this early in the morning a group of chattering schoolchildren were admiring the fossilized remains of the once-mighty masters of Earth, supervised by their teacher, a ServoRobot of a much later and sleeker design than Kili.

Shari felt very inferior as she gazed up at the reconstructed skeleton of a Tyrannosaurus rex, dwarfed by its huge size.

"Isn't he wonderful?" she gushed to Kristas who clearly thought it wasn't.

"It's just a heap of old bones," he said dismissively, and looked at the plaque at the front of the display. "Sixty-five million year old bones at that too. What's so wonderful about that?"

"Kristas!" Shari tut-tutted. "Tyrannosaurus rex was the largest flesh-eating animal ever to walk the face of the Earth," she explained. "It stood about twenty feet high and weighed over eight tonnes."

Kristas smiled at Shari's enthusiasm. "I wouldn't have liked to have been a caveman getting in its way then."

"Don't be an idiot, Kristas," Shari laughed. "Human beings weren't around 65 million years ago."

"Silly me, I should have known."

He stood aside to let the ServoRobot and its charges pass by. For a brief second the robot stopped and stared at Kristas' face before moving on to the Brachiosauruses at the far end of the room.

"It was only when the dinosaur died out that mammals on Earth had a chance of evolving into intelligent creatures," Shari continued. "Before then they were too busy trying to avoid becoming T. rex's next meal!"

"Just as well for us that they did die out then," he said.

"But no one knows why," Shari said, and looked thoughtfully up at the skeleton, as if it might somehow give her a clue. "They were the most successful species that ever lived on Earth—"

"Home Planet," Kristas reminded her in a whisper. "Remember where we are – we don't know who might be listening..."

"They were the most successful species ever to have lived on Home Planet," Shari said, "and then all of a sudden they just died out."

"Why?"

Shari shrugged. "I told you, no one really knows. Some people say that the Earth was struck by a meteorite or a comet. The resulting dust clouds from the impact blotted out the sun for years. The poor dinosaurs simply froze to death."

"Then what about the mammals?" asked Kristas, who was becoming intrigued by the story.

"Their fur kept them warm," she said. "Still, I'd love to know what really killed the dinosaurs off. But I suppose it'll always be a mystery."

"And I know another mystery that will never be solved," said Kristas, and took her by the hand into an adjoining display room.

The ServoRobot watched them go, and then

hustled its schoolchildren out of the room. Neither Shari nor Kristas saw the ServoRobot pause for a moment, regarding them thoughtfully. Finally it followed its charges out of the room, but not before having alerted the museum's authorities to the presence of Shari and Kristas.

Unlike the dinosaur hall the room Kristas had taken them into was empty. Shari guessed that while the dinosaurs might inspire people's imagination, few New Canberrans would be interested in a room whose main exhibits comprised a collection of rocks brought from the Home Planet.

She affected a yawn as Kristas consulted the plan of the room which was hung on the wall and then led her to one particular display case. She peered into the case: on a cushion of velvet there lay a large chunk of black rock. Running through it was a seam of silvery-white metal, which glittered in the overhead lights. She read the identification card on the case.

"'The Mexico Stone'," she said, and looked at Kristas, intrigued. "Dinosaurs bore you, but you're interested in a lump of rock from old Central America?"

Kristas's eyes shone. "That lump of rock is sixty-five million years old," he said, reading from the card.

"Just like the dinosaurs then," said Shari, greatly unimpressed.

"But do they have a streak of parondite running

right through them?" he asked, pointing to the silvery-white seam.

Shari shook her head and frowned: she couldn't see the importance of an impurity in the rock, no matter how prettily it glittered in the light.

"Parondite is a super-strong alloy we use in spacecraft construction, among other things," he continued.

"If you say so." Shari couldn't understand why Kristas was so interested.

"It was first manufactured about two or three hundred years ago."

Shari shrugged.

"So what ..." A sudden realization hit her. "*Two hundred years ago?*"

Kristas nodded. "That's right."

"Then if that rock is sixty-five million years old ..." Shari examined the display more closely now. "How did the parondite get in there?"

"Like the death of your dinosaurs no one really knows," Kristas admitted. "It could be the result of a freak geological accident..."

Shari smiled. "But you'd like to think it was something else?"

"Who knows? Maybe the Earth was visited by aliens."

"The Seti?"

He shrugged. "Or something else," he said.

Shari was about to question him further when she

was aware of a disturbance in the dinosaur hall. She and Kristas went through the doorway.

The schoolchildren were gone, but their Servo-Robot was still there, with the four security guards it had called in. They were all dressed in black combat gear, their heads covered in black helmets. Their guns were all trained on Shari and Kristas.

Shari and Kristas turned to run back into the rock room, but their way was barred by another armed guard who had seemingly appeared from nowhere; the badges on his leather jacket identified him as the chief guard. He swaggered up to them and waved his gun menacingly in their faces.

"Shari Sharifi? Kristas Chernenko?" he barked.

Shari and Kristas meekly nodded their heads.

"You are charged with stealing a skimmer and a ServoRobot," he began.

"I didn't steal Kili!" Shari began to protest before Kristas urged her to stop: they were in enough trouble already without Shari losing her temper with the security chief.

"But they have to know the truth!" she said, and was about to continue when the chief guard slapped her viciously in the face, so hard that she almost fell over. She massaged her cheek, more shocked than pained, and noticed that a thin trickle of blood was pouring from the side of her mouth.

"More from you, my pretty one," the guard

snarled, "and you'll be sorry." Shari glared at him but the inference was clear and she kept quiet.

"And furthermore for journeying off-world without due authorization, the falsification of official System transponder codes and entering TerraNova without credentials or adequate identification."

He nodded over to his colleagues who came forward and roughly grabbed them.

"Take 'em away and lock 'em up, lads," he said, and then smiled a long cruel grin before adding sadistically: "And don't worry, kids – you won't be locked up for long..."

Shari and Kristas exchanged grim, knowing looks as they were marched away. If what Cruse had told them was true, and it seemed increasingly likely that it was, then there was going to be little chance of them ever leaving TerraNova alive.

As they were dragged away neither of them noticed the old man in the shadows who had been watching them and following them ever since they had entered the museum. He took a small communicator out of his pocket and muttered a few whispered words into it.

Like the other inhabitants of New Canberra he was dressed in the standard-issue olive-green uniform, but if Shari had seen him she might have recognized him as Quester, the man she and Cruse had met on Avernus.

There was a worried look on Quester's aged face.

Damn those children! he cursed. Why did they have to come to the museum! Why did that blasted ServoRobot have to recognize their faces from System files!

This was not something that Quester had prepared for, this was not something which was part of his plan. It was going to be necessary to call in help.

Jarrl

$\mathcal{S}$ hari and Kristas shuddered as they heard the shrieks and caterwauls echoing down the long cold corridors of the detention centre. From far off there came blood-curdling cries of pain and anguish: it was a cruelly stark contrast to the warm and idyllic nature of the wide boulevards and small gardens of New Canberra. Indeed they could hardly believe that they were still in the capital city of TerraNova.

Of course, in the System this sort of detention centre wasn't supposed to exist, Shari had remarked wryly to Kristas; after all everyone was supposed to be perfectly contented with their lot, weren't they?

From the museum complex they had been taken by the security guards in an unmarked air jet to the detention centre which lay in the rocky wastes a few kilometres to the north of New Canberra.

There they had been unceremoniously dumped into a small featureless and windowless room, and the door locked behind them. That had been many long hours ago, and still they had had no indication of what their fate would be. The long wait was beginning to get to them, as indeed it was intended to. The System realized that after a few days in confinement, with only each other for company, they would be more than ready to talk and answer any questions that might be thrown at them. The only evidence of any life beyond the four walls of their tiny prison was a video camera which constantly scanned their cell.

Kristas was sitting on a small pallet, his head buried in his hands. He looked up at Shari who was pacing the room, searching in vain for a means of escape.

"How could they track us down, Shari?" he asked. "In a city of so many millions?"

"Who knows?" she said. "Maybe that robot we saw in the dinosaur room," she suggested. "We'll have been missed on Pasiphae by now. The System could have sent out a general alert."

"But why? What's so important about us that they want to track us all the way to Mars?"

Shari stared up into the video camera, at the people she knew must be watching them. She pulled a face at the camera: so what if it's childish – it feels good!

"We broke the law," she said. "The System doesn't want any disruptive elements."

Kristas wasn't convinced. "The ShantyLanders back on Pasiphae are disruptive elements," he said. "And yet the System seems content to let them live out in the Wastelands."

"Maybe it's not who we are at all," said Shari. "Maybe it's the time we're travelling – and where we're travelling to..."

"You mean the Seti?"

Shari nodded slowly. "We're at a turning point in history – the first ever contact with a completely alien species," she said. "But why do I get the feeling that I'm missing something vitally important?"

She sat down on the pallet next to Kristas and recalled a conversation she had had with Kili several years ago.

She had asked where all the minerals and gases, mined on Jupiter and Saturn, were taken to. Usually, when asked similar questions, Kili had told her to find out the answer herself and had directed her to an encyclopaedia or a relevant vid-disk in the Academy's library. This time, however, he had been much more forthcoming.

He had told her that while some of the minerals were taken to TerraNova to help in the continued terraforming of that planet, most were taken to Earth. Shari had remarked at the time that it was the first time that she had heard Kili using the word "Earth" rather than the officially recognized name of the Home Planet.

She had pressed the robot on the subject but all he would offer her were some ambiguous words about a mysterious engineering project. She had asked whether her father had had something to do with the project, at which point Kili had reminded her gently that her father was dead.

When Shari had persisted the robot deftly changed the subject, but not before remarking, "You'll learn all about it in time, Shari, I promise. Be patient: it's only a matter of time."

She turned to Kristas. "We're looking for my father, aren't we?" she said, and then corrected herself: "Well, I am anyway. And we think he's on Earth, or at least one of the Islands circling the planet."

"And the System – or someone – is trying to keep us away from Earth?" asked Kristas. "But what for?"

Shari sighed: she had no idea. And what did it matter anyway?

In a few hours they would probably both be dead.

Cruse turned his attention away from Doob, who was struggling in his arms, and glowered at Kili. "If you're wrong, robot..."

"I assure you that I am never wrong," Kili said huffily, outraged that his abilities were being called into question. "I am able to tap into the mainframe computer network which is shared by all System robots—"

"You're not supposed to be able to do that, robot," Cruse reminded him.

Kili gave him the cybernetic equivalent of an embarrassed cough. "Obviously I have been modified somewhat."

"Obviously."

"And I have learnt where Shari and Kristas are being held," Kili said. "It is imperative that they be rescued."

Cruse looked curiously at Kili. "Why are you so concerned about what happens to them, robot?" he asked. "You're nothing more than two and a half tons of metal and microchips. You've no emotions. You shouldn't care whether they live or die."

"I am programmed to ensure that Shari comes to no harm," came the terse reply. "And I note that you also care."

Cruse turned away. The robot is right! he admitted reluctantly to himself. Those kids have spirit – we're all going to need that if...

Cruse didn't allow himself to finish the thought. For all I know, that blasted robot can read minds as well! He seems to be able to do everything else he's not supposed to do!

"So how do you propose we rescue them?" asked Cruse. He reached down to the gun at his belt. "One blaster isn't going to breach System security, you know. We'd never get in."

"You have misunderstood me," said Kili in that infuriatingly superior voice of his. "The object is not to get ourselves in, but to get Shari and Kristas *out*."

Since Shari and Kristas had been locked in the cell no one had come to visit them, apart from one surly guard who had brought them some sparse food on a tray. When Shari had demanded what was going to happen to them he had simply shrugged his shoulders and refused to reply.

Now, hours later they were staring miserably and unseeing at the bleak and blank walls of the cell. Time seemed to have stood still – they had no idea whether it was day or night.

Shari stood up and listened; she thought she could hear something. A scratching coming from somewhere quite near.

"What's that noise?"

"Probably my stomach rumbling," complained Kristas.

Shari hushed him, and listened again. She looked up at the small ventilation grille set high in the far wall of their cell; the noise seemed to be coming from there.

By now Kristas could hear the noise as well, and he stood up, and, with Shari's help, moved the pallet underneath the ventilation grille.

"There's someone in there!" said Shari as she climbed on the pallet and stood on tip-toes to take a look through the grille. The grille was directly to the left of the video camera, and by standing on the pallet Shari was effectively out of camera shot.

"Don't be stupid," Kristas said scornfully. "No human being could fit into a ventilation shaft that small! He'd have to be a midget..."

Shari grinned, and put her long fingers through the grille. She pulled hard and the grille loosened. Taking a deep breath she pulled again, and the grille fell away, revealing the narrow ventilation shaft beyond.

"... Or a chimp!" said Shari as, with a joyful chirruping, Doob sprang out of the shaft and into Shari's arms. She cuddled her and stroked her fur, chattering to her as a mother would to a child. "Doobie, I don't know what you're doing here but it's good to see you, baby!"

Kristas jumped on the pallet too to stroke Doob. And then he noticed what Doob was carrying. Slung across Doob's shoulder was a blaster.

"Cruse ..." said Shari, and then fell silent.

Kristas was pointing up to the video camera; they were out of shot now, but the second they climbed off the pallet, their guards would be able to see everything which was happening in the cell.

Shari handed Doob over to Kristas, and took the gun off the chimp. Silently she indicated that Kristas should step off the pallet, and back into the range of the camera. She followed, carefully concealing the gun from the camera.

She went up to Kristas and tickled Doob on the ear. "Doobie baby, it's so good to see you again," she cooed loudly, hoping to attract the attention of the guards who, she knew, might not necessarily have been watching the video screen with their fullest attention.

"We knew you'd come in here and find us," said Kristas, quickly realizing what Shari was planning. "We knew the guards couldn't keep you out." He shot a look up at the video camera and added maliciously: "Intellectually you're a match for any of them."

"And much prettier too," joined in Shari. The whole point was to attract the watching guard's attention to the intruder in their cell, and Shari and Kristas didn't have to wait for long. Within a minute the door to their cell swished open and the surly guard who had brought their food strode in. He frowned, taking in at once the open ventilation shaft, and Shari and Kristas stroking their pet chimpanzee.

He didn't have time to take in much more.

In a flash Shari pulled Cruse's gun from behind her back. For a second she seemed uncertain how to operate the weapon, and then she flicked the trigger and fired at the guard. He screamed with pain as the blast hit him, as planned, in the legs and he crumpled to the floor.

His vision blurring with pain he still tried to reach the gun at the holster by his side, but Kristas was too quick for him. Dropping Doob to the floor, he jumped on top of the guard, wrestling the gun from his side. He leapt up and he and Shari both trained their guns on him. Kristas looked despairingly at the wounded guard.

"What do we do now?" he asked.

His hands were shaking as he pointed the gun at the guard; only a few days ago he was a respected interpreter working for the System: now here he was a fugitive gunman!

"I don't know!" snapped Shari, whose hands were also trembling.

She knew what Cruse would do: he would have shot the guard dead there and then in cold blood. But she wasn't a killer, and it had taken all her courage even to shoot the guard in the legs. Down on the floor, the guard glared at her, almost defying her to shoot him.

Shari nodded towards the open door. "Pick up Doob!" she commanded. "Let's get out of here!"

Kristas rushed out of the cell with Doob in his arms. Shari paused for a moment, mumbled an embarrassed "sorry" to the fallen guard, and ran out after him.

"Where to now?" asked Kristas, as he looked frantically up and down the corridor for some way out. When they had first been brought here, they had been taken down what had to them seemed to be miles upon miles of featureless grey corridors. Shari raced over to a small hover-buggy which the guards used to travel along the corridors of the detention centre.

Kristas clambered in after her. "Do you know how to work this thing?" he asked, in amazement.

"Of course not," Shari said cheerfully, as she flicked a switch on the dashboard and rested her hands on the steering wheel. The buggy buzzed into life, and started to move drunkenly forward as Shari tried to get the hang of the steering.

Suddenly the air was filled with the blare of a warning siren. The guard in their cell had obviously managed to drag himself to an emergency switch and sound the alarm.

The buggy was still moving at a snail's pace, and Shari looked down despairingly at the dashboard.

"How do I increase the speed on this blasted thing?" she asked. "The guards will be on us in no time if we keep on crawling at this pace!"

Kristas pointed to a pedal down by Shari's left foot. "Perhaps that?" he suggested.

Shari looked doubtful and shook her head. "I don't think so," she said, and continued to look at the dashboard.

There was a sudden commotion behind them, and they turned around. A group of seven or eight guards had come up behind them, guns raised ready to fire.

"Give yourself up now!" cried their leader, as the buggy moved slowly away from them.

One over eager guard fired two warning shots in the air. The sudden noise frightened Doob, and, with a terrified shriek, she jumped off Kristas's lap to hide herself on the floor of the buggy.

She landed on the pedal by Shari's foot, and suddenly the buggy shot off away from the guards down the corridor, with such a force that Shari and Kristas were thrown back into their seats.

"Doob, you're wonderful!" cried Shari and placed her foot on the accelerator pedal, increasing their speed even more. She tried not to look at Kristas whose lips were silently mouthing the words: *I told you so!* Behind them the guards were clambering into their own buggies, and giving chase.

When they had first been brought here both Shari and Kristas had had the impression that they were going down, guessing correctly that part of the detention centre was built underground, safe from the prying and curious eyes of law-abiding TerraNovans. So, in the absence of any knowledge of the geography of the centre, Shari simply continued to drive the buggy upwards, hoping that that would at least bring her to the exit and the surface.

The wail of the alarm siren still blared in their ears, drowning out the cries of the guards who were rapidly catching up with them. They were firing on them now and it was only Shari's erratic driving which caused them to avoid the majority of the bullets and blasts. A few bullets hit the buggy and pinged harmlessly off its metal exterior.

Suddenly the alarm stopped. For one brief second Shari and Kristas thought that they were safe, but a brief look around showed that the guards were still in hot pursuit. She rammed her foot even harder down on the accelerator pedal, and the buggy zoomed even further ahead.

Minutes later they reached a dead end, and jumped out of the buggy, with Kristas picking up the terrified Doob in his arms again. They were standing before two large and sturdy-looking doors; Kristas recognized them from before – he was sure they led to the surface and freedom. He threw his weight against them but they refused to budge. He looked down at the gun he had taken from the guard, wondering whether it would be powerful enough to blast a hole in the doors.

Shari shook her head. "They might work on people," she said, and ran her hand over the doors. "But these look as though they're made out of reinforced concrete…"

Kristas looked down the corridor. The guards' buggy was rapidly approaching them; they were trapped.

"Listen!" said Shari. Something – someone – was pounding on the other side of the doors.

The buggy was only fifteen metres away. Now that

they could see that their quarry was trapped, the guards had stopped firing.

The pounding increased on the concrete doors. Shari and Kristas looked expectantly at each other; in Kristas's arms Doob whimpered gently.

The guards were ten metres away now. Shari and Kristas could hear their cries and insults as they approached.

Louder and louder the pounding grew. A chink of light appeared in the crack where the two doors joined.

Five metres away now. Kristas could see the guards' triumphant faces, gloating at their predicament.

Crash!

The double doors opened inwards in a cloud of dust and shattered stone. Even the guards were taken aback as Kili pushed open the huge doors, and Shari rushed through the open doorway and hugged his huge metal frame.

"I simply do not know what you would do without me," Kili sighed dramatically.

By his side, Cruse grabbed his blaster off Shari and started firing on the approaching guards as Kristas and Doob rushed out into the open air.

"Get out of here!" he growled, as one by one the guards in the buggy fell down dead.

Shari hesitated for a minute, shocked by the killing.

"Where to?" she cried above the noise of Cruse's blaster.

"Just move!"

With Cruse giving them cover Shari, Kristas and Kili began to move away from the doors of the detention building towards the rocks and rubble at the foothills of Olympus Mons.

And then they stopped.

From their hiding places behind the rocks twenty or more armed guards appeared. They trained their guns on Shari's party; and a warning shot was fired in Cruse's direction. The mercenary stopped shooting, realizing that he was hopelessly outnumbered. One of the guards came forward and wrenched his blaster from his hand. Cruse spat in his face.

After the deafening noise of gunfire, everything was now uncannily still. One of the guards detached himself from the group and swaggered over to Shari and the others. She recognized him as the leader of the guards who had arrested them in the science museum earlier. He grinned at them.

"Thought you could get away, did you?" he slimed. "You don't escape the System that easy, you know."

"What are you going to do with us?" asked Shari, forcing herself to stare the oily man straight in the eye. It was an effort to keep her voice steady, but she was determined not to show that she was frightened.

"Kill you," came the simple reply.

"You can't do that!" protested Kristas, while by his side Cruse just lifted his eyes heavenwards and sighed at his companion's naïveté.

"Oh, can't I?" said the chief. "You've been found guilty of journeying off-world for purposes inimical to the System, and illegally entering TerraNovan space at a time of maximum security."

"We haven't even been put on trial yet!" Shari declared. "When were we found guilty, and by whom?"

The security chief smiled. "Just now. And by me." He walked up to Kili.

"And you, robot, should be ashamed of yourself, acting against your programming."

"I have no emotions," said Kili huffily. "Therefore I cannot be ashamed."

The security chief eyed the robot warily. "Of course not . . . but you're a strange one. We'll find out just how different you are when we take you apart."

Shari gasped at the thought of her old friend being dismantled, limb by limb.

The security chief then turned his attention to Kristas. He took Doob from his arms. In a stark and almost farcical change of mood the security chief cuddled the chimp to his breast.

"At least the chimp will go to a good home," he said. "I do soooo love animals." He stroked Doob's fur, at which point the animal bit him. With an angry and pained yelp, the security chief threw the animal to the ground and Doob scampered back to Kristas.

"OK, lads, this is it," he said. His colleagues raised their guns.

Shari looked wildly around. They were surrounded on three sides: their only possible escape route was back into the detention centre, and once in there they would be as good as dead.

"On the count of three..."

Shari clutched Kristas's arm. Her best friend was trembling almost as much as she was.

"One..."

She felt Cruse's firm hand on her shoulder: it felt strangely comforting and reassuring.

"Crazy kids," he murmured. "If not for you I wouldn't be in this mess now."

"Two..."

Shari shut her eyes, preparing herself for the impact.

Cruse meanwhile just stared at the security chief, determined that the fat oily man would never forget his dying look of hatred and contempt.

The guards glanced expectantly at their leader. The security chief paused, clearly enjoying prolonging the execution as much as possible.

He opened his mouth to issue the final order to fire.

"Stop! There will be no more killing!"

The security chief turned around to see a burly middle-aged man step out from behind the rocks. He was accompanied by a much older man with a shock of white hair who was walking with the aid of a cane.

"Put down your guns," the middle-aged man continued. "I am now assuming responsibility for these people."

Disappointed, the security chief ordered his men to lay down their weapons, as the two older men approached him. His fellow guards muttered amongst themselves: it was plain that they recognized the two older men.

Cruse breathed a sigh of relief, and glanced at his companions. The lights on Kili's chest unit were twinkling frantically: if he didn't know better (and by now Cruse wasn't sure that he did) he could have sworn that the robot was chuckling to itself.

Kristas was regarding the two newcomers with a look of sheer and wide-eyed disbelief. In his arms Doob burbled excitedly to herself.

Shari still had her eyes closed, scarcely able to believe what was happening and scared to open them for fear that it was all a dream.

At her side she felt Kristas nudge her gently.

"Open your eyes, Shari," he said softly. "Take a look..."

Slowly Shari opened her eyes which were already misted with tears.

Before her was Jarrl, the father she had not seen for nine long years.

Five Days to Earth

The egg-shaped craft slowed down as it veered a course away from TerraNova and the planet's security and defence craft, which its pilots suspected might impede their safe passage to their destination. Younger members of the crew had suggested that they had nothing to fear from the humans; after all, for a race to advance to the point which humanity had, must mean that they were essentially civilized and peaceful. Older members, however, had argued for caution: their mission of mass destruction must not be allowed to fail at the last stage.

The navigator returned from his rest period and studied the ship's route on the screen before him. Like every other piece of equipment on board the ship the navigation panel had not been manufactured, but *grown* on their own planet. As such, it had a natural affinity with the pilots of the ship, whose psychic powers were considerable.

The screen showed TerraNova, and beyond that the Old Earth. That was their destination, he thought with satisfaction, that was where the Great Dying would begin. The navigator chuckled at the images on his screen.

The navigator returned from his rest period and studied the ship's route on the screen before him.

The navigator returned from his rest period and studied the ship's route on the screen before him...

The navigator returned...

The navigator shook his head, and grunted, his nostrils flaring as he attempted to catch his breath back. The younger members of the crew were less affected by these timeslips, but at just over a thousand years old he was rapidly approaching middle-age. This was the third time such a thing had happened to him, and each time the effect was more disorientating.

Still, reflected the navigator, that was only to be expected in a race as time-sensitive as his. The closer they got to the Old Earth, so the more frequently these spasms would occur. The people of Earth, even if they didn't suspect it, were about to stumble onto the basic principles of time technology.

And it was essential that they handed that technology over to the Seti.

Even if it did mean mass suicide, the Seti pilot thought, and steered the craft on its course towards Earth.

PART 3

The Seti

Four Days to Earth

The image of the Island loomed large on the video screen and the navigator was genuinely impressed with the humans' technology. He looked over at the two drones who were skulking in a darkened corner of the navigation chamber. How different these two were from the humans on the Islands! These bipeds the Seti had brought with them across light years of space showed very little intelligence, and were content merely to perform the tasks which were given them by their masters. Bred in the Seti's own laboratories they were, the navigator decided, primitive in the extreme.

A bloodshot eye swivelled ninety degrees to register a warning bleep on one of the instruments. The navigator sighed a long guttural sigh and relayed the information to its colleagues on board the egg-shaped craft.

The space station was armed. That meant that they could not simply pass it by on their way to their destination; their mission was too vital to risk their craft being destroyed by one of the humans' missiles. They would have to communicate once more with those absurd little creatures!

The navigator operated the control which sent out a stream of radio waves towards the space station. The navigator doubted very much whether the primitive creatures on the Island would be able to decipher the message; but if they could, they would hear the Seti proclaiming that they meant no harm to any living creature at all.

The Seti only hoped that the humans would believe them. That was the trouble with inferior creatures, it realized: one could never predict just how they would act in any given circumstance. If the humans chose not to believe them, and to regard them instead as a threat to their existence then the Seti's plans would all be in vain.

Wearily the navigator adjusted the controls and directed the egg-shaped craft towards the space station.

The navigator sighed. He knew it was wrong to feel this way but he did so hate dealing with inferior beings.

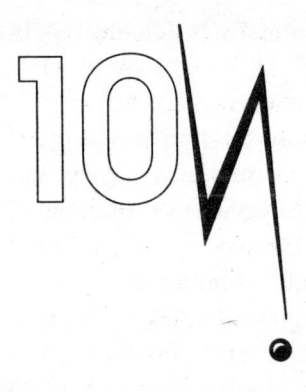

The Island

$\mathcal{S}$ hari stared strangely at her father, still not quite believing that they had finally been reunited after nine years. He looked much as she remembered him, even though his once jet-black hair was now streaked with grey, and there were lines about his eyes; more lines than would be normal in a forty-five-year-old man. They had been together for over a day now, and Shari was convinced that she was going to wake up soon and find it had all been a dream.

When Jarrl had suddenly appeared outside the detention centre, the security chief had immediately dismissed his guards and hurriedly departed. It seemed to Shari that her father carried some sort of authority here; but Cruse, whose judgement was not clouded by emotion, suspected that the real authority lay in the wizened white-haired man at Jarrl's side. He frowned, trying to remember where he had seen him before.

Shari, meanwhile, had just hugged her father to her, determined never to let him go again. She looked up into his face: he was smiling, but there was a sad expression in his eyes.

"I knew you were alive, Daddy," she sobbed. "Even when Kili said you were dead."

Jarrl glanced guiltily over to the robot who remained infuriatingly silent. "I had to leave you," he said, and his voice was shaking.

"But why?" she asked.

"There were reasons ..." Jarrl looked over at the old man, remembering the veiled threats he had made if Jarrl refused to co-operate with the System. Jarrl realized that the System was corrupt, and hated being forced to work for it, but he had loved his daughter even more and could not allow her to be hurt. "I've been with you every hour of the day."

Shari nodded. "I think I knew all along," she said, recalling the times when she had been sure her vidphone was on, watching her. She remembered also the small gifts which Kili had often presented her with, without mentioning their provenance.

What she couldn't know – and what Jarrl wasn't prepared to reveal to her – was that he had enjoyed a direct link with Kili's visual circuitry; Shari's father had access to everything that Kili had seen over the past nine years. He had seen his daughter growing up, seen her studying late at night, and had known about her flight from Pasiphae.

Jarrl held out his hand to Kristas, who had been watching this family reunion with a feeling of awkwardness.

"Thank you for looking after Shari for me, Kristas," he said.

"No problem, sir."

The old man stepped forward. "If you are ready, Jarrl, I think we had better be leaving for the Island..."

Shari was panic-stricken. Surely she wasn't going to be separated from her father again so soon after they had been reunited?

The old man smiled. "Of course Shari and Kristas may accompany you," he said. He looked down at Doob, who was happily hugging Jarrl's legs. "And the monkey too, I suppose," he sighed.

Shari looked over at Cruse. "What about Cruse?" she asked anxiously.

A look passed between the old man and the mercenary. Cruse now realized who the old man reminded him of. He had never seen him before without a mask but he still recognized the voice of Quester, the con-man from Avernus who had provided them with the means to get to TerraNova.

Cruse suddenly had the feeling that they were all being manipulated: it was not a feeling he liked. But for the moment he was content to keep his thoughts to himself.

Quester nodded, fully aware that Cruse knew who he was. "Your friend may come too, Shari," he said.

"Thank you, Lord Quester," said Jarrl.

Lord Quester? thought Cruse. A high-ranking System official then? Or something more?

"My pleasure," said Quester, and pointed beyond the rocks. "Our shuttle is just over there. We can be on the Island in a matter of hours."

Shari's party began to follow Quester, leaving Kili standing alone. Quester turned around.

"Well come along, Kilimanjaro," he said tetchily. "We haven't got all day!"

"I was merely waiting to be invited," Kili said grumpily, and followed the others.

Cruse slapped the robot on the back in a gesture of mock camaraderie. "And waiting to be introduced as well, I suppose," he said. "Shari never introduced you to Quester, did she, robot?"

"That is correct."

"So how did he know your name?"

Kili "coughed". "Perhaps Jarrl told him my name...."

And perhaps he didn't, thought Cruse.

"Why did you leave me, Daddy?" Shari asked again, as the shuttle steered into docking orbit around the

Island, the space station which orbited the Home Planet.

Jarrl turned his face away from the viewport and looked at his daughter with unshed tears in his eyes.

"Things were so different then," he said. "The System needed my help, my expertise on a ... project down there." He indicated the rusty-brown globe of the Earth, which made a stark contrast to the gleaming whiteness of the orbiting Island.

"And you had to leave me, let me think that you were dead ..." Shari continued, an almost accusatory tone in her voice.

"You don't understand, Shari," her father said. "The System gave me no choice. They needed me as a member of their scientific elite." He laughed ironically, ruefully. "You must do what the System tells you to do – if you want to survive, that is."

"I didn't," Shari pointed out. "I broke the rules and came looking for you."

Jarrl turned guiltily away. He knew what Shari was thinking, that he was weak-willed and cowardly; but there were things she couldn't understand.

He remembered Mad Marla. She had been his student all those long years ago. And alone of the lecturers at the Academy he had seen her body when it was dragged out of that tiny, windowless room. He had seen that face, once so animated and fresh and alive, now grey and lifeless, all its youth and intelligence and promise blasted out of it by the guns of the System.

It was then that he realized what the System was capable of, had known that they would show no hesitation in doing the same to Shari if he refused to work for them. By leaving Shari in the care of Kili he told himself he was saving her life. If only she could realize that, but even after all her adventures she could still not see the full extent of the System's power and viciousness.

Shari continued to stare at her father, still loving him but beginning to see him in a new light. Suddenly she was aware of the great gap between them, the gap that separated those who worked for the System for whatever reason, and those, like herself, Kristas and Cruse, who dared to ask questions, who dared to say no.

"And Kili has looked after you well in the last few years, hasn't he?"

Shari nodded. "He's been my best friend, after Kristas," she said, but still pressed on: "Is it Quester? Are you frightened of him in some way? He was the man who came to see you the night you went away, wasn't he?"

Jarrl laughed awkwardly. "Afraid of Quester?"

"Are you?"

Jarrl shook his head, but Shari wasn't completely convinced. "He's a powerful man, though," Jarrl said. "Almost three hundred years old..."

Shari whistled. The longevity drugs produced some centuries ago could increase a human being's natural life span to approximately two hundred and twenty years, but she had never heard of anyone living to Quester's advanced age before.

"They say he was one of the last people to be born on Old Earth – I mean the Home Planet," Jarrl hastily corrected himself. "He rose among the ranks from practically nowhere to a position of influence in the System. What's more, he's supposedly also close friends with both the President and Donovan True-heart."

"Donovan Trueheart?" The name meant little to Shari.

"Leader of the EarthLifers, and the head of System Security," her father said. He looked around to make sure no one was listening. "An odious man if you ask me. But you can make up your own mind; you'll be meeting him soon."

"He's on the Island?" Shari asked. The shuttle on which they were travelling shuddered as it docked with the space station.

"Everyone who is anyone is," said Jarrl. "Politicians, scientists, Trueheart, the President herself. And for some reason Quester has allowed you and your friends – and Kili, of course – to be there as well..."

"Why?"

"Haven't you heard?" asked Jarrl, and suddenly he sounded once again like the father she used to know, letting her in on a great secret. "Quester has arranged that you've all been given security clearance. You're all going to meet the Seti!"

The corridors of the Island gleamed white and antiseptic, as Quester led Shari and her friends to their quarters. As they walked down the corridors technicians and officials would stop to look at them before continuing on their way.

And there's a lot to stare at! Shari realized. She and Kristas hadn't had a change of clothes or a bath in days, and Cruse in his worn and dirty leathers looked distinctly out of place in the tidy clean environment of the space station. Kili, as a Mark Seven robot, was approximately one hundred and fifty years out of date, and she wondered if the Administrators of the Island had ever seen a chimpanzee like Doob before, let alone allowed one on board.

"I'm sure you will all be comfortable in your new quarters," said Quester.

"I'd feel a lot more comfortable with my blaster," grumbled Cruse, whose gun had been taken away from him as soon as they had left the Island's docking bay.

Quester tut-tutted. "We are all friends here on the Island," said Quester. "The System provides and we are content."

Cruse glared at him. What game are you playing, Quester?

"Why ever would you need a gun here?" Quester continued in an infuriatingly patronizing tone of voice.

"To shoot a few of those blasted Seti if they get out of hand," he replied.

"Is that all you think about?" asked Kristas angrily. "Shooting anything you don't understand?"

"I wouldn't like to think that you're becoming an EarthLifer, Cruse," chuckled Quester. Cruse growled at him.

"EarthLifers?" asked Shari.

"A bunch of religious fanatics," offered Cruse.

"Who are also one of the most influential political parties on TerraNova," added Quester, "and the followers of the great and glorious Donovan Trueheart." There was a touch of irony and even disrespect in the old man's voice. He activated a touch-sensitive control and a door swished open, leading to the Island's living quarters.

"They believe that Mankind is only one step away from the angels," said Kili. "And that the Seti are a threat to your existence."

"And you, of course, don't believe that, do you, Cruse?" Quester smiled.

"I've an open mind," he admitted. "But I also believe that until we know why they're here we don't give them the benefit of the doubt!"

"I've been thinking a lot about them," said Kristas.

"And?"

"And I'm beginning to think that they must be peaceful..."

"And how do you make that out, dreamer?"

"If they have the technology to travel across half a galaxy—"

"Something which we don't have," said Quester, and added meaningfully: "Yet."

"—then they must be so civilized that war is total anathema to them." He looked over to Shari for support. "Isn't that right, Shari?"

Shari, however, remained silent, once again remembering her studies of Earth history.

"We thought we were 'civilized' in the 24th century," Cruse reminded them. "And look what happened – a war that wiped out two-thirds of the world's population and laid waste one and a half continents. Only the people who got into the bunkers and underground shelters in time survived. So much for civilization!"

Shari looked oddly at Cruse. She knew that there had been a great war on Earth all those hundreds of years ago, but this was the first time she had heard anything about people surviving in underground shelters.

"Shelters?" she asked.

"That's right," said Cruse. "Thousands of them dotted all over the planet." Then he added hurriedly: "Of course, they've all been destroyed now."

Kristas looked suspiciously at Cruse. "Just like the

tunnels under Pasiphae leading to ShantyLand?" he asked. "The System told us that they had been destroyed as well, but you found a way through them..."

Cruse glared at him.

Quester smiled. "Well, you will all soon find out whether the Seti are peaceful or not," he said amiably.

"What d'you mean?" asked Shari.

"The Seti are now in visual range of our scanners," Quester explained. "In little more than two days' time they will be here!"

Two Days to Earth

The navigator's claws skimmed quickly over the controls as he guided the egg-shaped craft into docking position. Twenty pairs of bloodshot and rheumy eyes gazed expectantly at the image on the video screen as the Seti craft approached the Island. They all had to concentrate especially hard: the time-distortions which they had felt ever since they had entered Earth's solar system were becoming stronger and more frequent now.

The captain of the ship laid a claw on the navigator's shoulder, dripping acidic slime down the navigator's back. His voice was raspy and rough.

Is the space station armed?

The navigator assured him that the Island was indeed armed, but that its defence mechanisms were only on standby. It seemed that the humans were ready to welcome them first, before deciding whether to shoot them out of the skies.

The captain chuckled. The question had been asked out of simple curiosity. The Seti had nothing to fear from mankind. They were so far advanced in comparison to the humans, and had planned for every eventuality hundreds of years beforehand, that they could immobilize every single one of the space station's defence systems with just the mere flick of a switch. Yet there was a reason for them coming to the Island...

He glanced over at another of his companions, a youngster only seven hundred years old, who was hunched over a huge purple-fronded plant. The plant had been specially bred in the Seti's nurseries and was sensitive to the minutest changes in atmosphere. The edges of the leaves were flecked with green, and the youngster conveyed to her captain the meaning of the colour change.

The humans breathe an atmosphere largely composed of oxygen, she told him. The Seti, whose normal atmosphere consisted of ammonia and methane, would have to adapt their respiratory systems accordingly. It was no great problem; after all, even the lowly drones had been bred to respond to a variety of hostile environments.

The navigator slowly brought their craft into dock with the Island. The atmosphere on board the Seti ship was electric. Soon the Seti and the humans would meet for the first time.

And then, soon after that first meeting, the Great Dying would begin.

The Seti

The atmosphere on board the space station was electric.

Almost the entire crew of the Island had gathered in the station's huge main docking bay to greet the Seti. Those who were unable to attend were watching the whole event on the hundreds of video screens dotted around the space station.

Shari and her party had been ushered into a corner away from the main welcoming committee. From there Kili pointed out some of the figures waiting to greet the aliens.

There was the System President, a tall imposing woman with short black hair, dressed in a long and flowing green robe. From time to time Quester would go up to her with news of the Seti's progress.

By the President's side was the great Donovan Trueheart, the charismatic leader of the EarthLifers. Kili had explained that Trueheart had insisted that he be present here at this great occasion; the President recognized too well the power of the EarthLifers to refuse him this request.

What neither of them knew was that Trueheart had ensured his presence at the President's side by reminding her of her past financial indiscretions. He had told her that he would hate it if the other members of the System found out about it; after all the System's ruling members were renowned for their back-stabbing and naked ambition. Even without knowing that Trueheart was a blackmailer Shari found that she took an instant dislike to the man.

Cruse growled when he recognized Trueheart as the man responsible for the deaths of Marla and the others all those years ago, but he kept his silence. Trueheart wouldn't remember him, he realized: after all, Cruse was just one of the many "deaths" Trueheart had been responsible for over the years.

In addition to the President and Trueheart, there were several people whose faces Shari vaguely recognized from news bulletins, plus a host of white-coated technicians and scientists. Discreetly mingled in the crowd were also black-suited guards, their guns primed and ready; they were members of System Security and, as such, fell under Donovan Trueheart's direct command.

"Well, at least someone's showing some sort of common sense," Cruse had muttered as they were ushered into the docking bay.

All eyes were focused on a massive pair of double doors, which led to the airlock. It was through these doors that the Seti would emerge after their craft had docked.

By Shari's side Kristas could hardly contain his excitement. This was what he had dreamt about ever since he was first approached by the Board on Pasiphae, and he could hardly believe he was here at one of the most important points in the history of Mankind.

His excitement was shared by all the others in the docking bay. What would the Seti look like? What secrets would they reveal to mankind? These were the questions which everyone was asking each other. Several others were also asking much more apprehensively: *What do they want with us?*

A deep rumbling filled the room. All eyes turned to the President. A technician came up to her and whispered some words in her ear. She nodded and then addressed the assembled crowd.

"The Seti craft has now docked with the Island," she announced grandly. "Within minutes we will no longer be alone in the Universe. Within minutes we will come face-to-face with another intelligent race. Let us treat them with the respect and co-operation we would wish to be given to ourselves."

There was a general murmur of agreement among the crowd; most people seemed to be on the side of the President. However there was at least one voice of dissent.

"But let us not forget that we are creation's chosen people," spoke up Donovan Trueheart in his thin and reedy voice which nevertheless carried a true sense of power. "Our destiny as the supreme creature of creation must never be forgotten or weakened."

The President shot Trueheart a withering look, but knew better than to reply to the EarthLifer and offend his many influential supporters in the crowd. Jarrl came up to her, and passed her some information.

"Our instruments say that the atmosphere on board the Seti craft is composed of ammonia and methane," she announced.

There was some consternation among the spectators, each one wondering what sort of creatures could survive in such a poisonous atmosphere.

"There will therefore be an unfortunate delay while we—"

The President frowned as Quester came up to her with even more news. "The Seti craft has opened its airlock ... Our friends from the stars are coming through now."

The tension in the air was almost tangible but it was underscored by another emotion, one of apprehension and indeed of awe. The Seti survived on ammonia and methane; and yet already they had adjusted their respiratory systems to breathe oxygen. They had travelled across light years of space when Mankind had not yet reached beyond the outermost planet Pluto. What else might they be capable of?

Donovan Trueheart winced: the Seti's powers of adaption were already undermining his long-held credo that Mankind was the highest and most evolved living creature. The discovery that the Seti might even be *superior* to Mankind could threaten his ever-growing power base on TerraNova.

The President received another report from one of her aides. The Seti had left their ship, she was told; they were now on the other side of the airlock door.

She sneaked a look up at the video technician who was positioned on an overhead gallery, recording the entire scene for the World News Network. He was checking and rechecking his camera equipment in order to ensure that he got the best shot possible of the President greeting the aliens.

Satisfied that everything was fine, he nodded his permission: the President could now welcome the Seti on board the Island.

"Fellow citizens of the System," she said. "For thousands of years Mankind has been alone. Now we are no longer. Now we welcome our brothers in space with open arms. Let the Seti come aboard!"

The double doors of the airlock sighed open. For a second everyone was overcome with the sharp and acrid stink of ammonia, the residue from the Seti's ship.

And then they saw the Seti.

They were horrific; the stuff of the wildest nightmares.

Shari grabbed Kristas's arms in terror: none of them had ever expected anything like this. Even Cruse's face was ashen, and his hand automatically reached for his gun – the gun which had been taken away from him.

Even the normally cool-headed President was taken aback and in the crowd Donovan Trueheart nodded sagely, as all his worst fears were suddenly confirmed.

Indeed, the only two persons not to register any shock or horror were Kili, who regarded the Seti with the impassivity only a supposedly emotionless robot was capable of, and Quester himself, who allowed himself the merest suspicion of a smile.

The smallest of the five Seti who had come aboard was a little over seven feet tall; the tallest towered almost nine feet. Their lithe reptilian bodies were covered with green scales, on which glistened a silvery-grey mucus which trailed behind them like the slime left by a slug. They staggered through the doorway and their clawed feet scraped and scratched on the metallic floor.

Their red eyes shot sharply about them as they surveyed their reception committee, and they hissed, displaying rows of razor sharp teeth and forked tongues. The nostrils in their snouts flared while they tried to adjust to the oxygen-rich atmosphere of the space station.

Shari gazed on in horror as she tried to think what they reminded her of. And then she realized.

Dinosaurs, she thought. Dinosaur embryos on two legs!

The tallest of the Seti stepped forward and approached the President who instinctively recoiled. Like all the other Seti he was naked apart from an orange band which hung around his stumpy neck, and which seemed to serve as some sort of badge of office: he was obviously the leader of the group. He opened his mouth, out of which came a strange unearthly growl.

Donovan Trueheart made an almost imperceptible gesture to one of the armed guards who was standing near Shari's group. The guard gave out what appeared to be a terrified shout, and let loose a series of shots onto the alien, the first of which struck the tall Seti on its shoulder.

Instantly one of its companions flung itself in front of its leader to take the full force of the shots. The bullets slammed mercilessly into its body, and fountains of dark red blood spurted from its wounds. It fell to the floor with a sickening thud.

"Stop that man!" screamed the President.

Several of her personal guards overpowered the

gunman, bringing him and his weapon down to the ground. In the crowd Donovan Trueheart stroked his chin and smiled; Mankind would never live peaceably with a bunch of overgrown crocodiles, he realized, and began to wonder just how he could turn this to his advantage.

For long seconds the four remaining Seti stared at the humans. Their bloodshot eyes were full of hate for the people who had just murdered one of their colleagues.

Finally the President stepped out of the crowd.

"We mean you no harm," she said, in direct contradiction of what had just happened. "We ... apologize for this unfortunate incident."

The four Seti growled threateningly at her, but made no move towards her.

The President nervously called to her side one of the Island's linguists, one of the Academicians who had won one of the places which Kristas had coveted. He repeated the President's words in several Earth-based languages, and then in four different sign languages. The Seti showed no understanding whatsoever.

The absurdity of the situation struck Kristas first of all. How could two totally alien species, with completely different backgrounds, hope ever to communicate intelligently with each other? As with so many other things the System had simply not considered the implications of this first contact with the Seti.

Once again the tallest Seti tried to speak. Globs of thick, acidic saliva dripped from its mouth and fell, steaming, onto the floor. Several people turned their faces away in disgust. Shari felt the bile rise in her throat.

People of Earth, we greet you, the Seti said. Its voice was low and guttural.

Shari looked curiously up at Kristas; his face was beaming with wonder. "How can they speak our language?" she asked him, and then realized that the words she and everyone else could hear were not coming from the creature's mouth.

"Telepathy," he whispered. "Of course: it's the only way two alien species can effectively communicate with each other."

Kristas whistled appreciatively: he had seen crude demonstrations of telepathy before back at the Academy on Pasiphae; but they were little more than glorified side shows, tentative experiments into Mankind's presumed psychic abilities. They had never been on a scale such as this.

The Seti looked down at its dead comrade.

You have destroyed one of our kind, it stated simply.

Although its eyes still burned hatefully there was no anger in its voice: it was merely reporting the facts.

The President stepped forward, trying hard to disguise the revulsion she so obviously felt towards the aliens; even the smell of them made her want to vomit.

"That was a regrettable accident," she claimed. "The perpetrator will be punished."

There is no need, came the reply. *The killer's fear was ... understandable ... It is said that inferior races always fear that which is different to themselves. The Seti are pacifist, and regard all life as sacred. But we have encountered similar instances of irrationality before in inferior creatures such as our drones...*

As if on cue, two ape-like creatures emerged from the airlock. Their bodies were hairy and they looked warily at the assembled humans.

For a second Shari was reminded of Doob. Then she saw the hard gleam of intelligence in their eyes and changed her mind: these "drones" resembled nothing more than the pictures of Neanderthal men she had seen in her college textbooks.

They are our helpers, the Seti said in reply to the unspoken question.

"Or your slaves?"

Everyone turned to see who had spoken: it was Donovan Trueheart.

They have no will of their own, said the Seti. *They are grown in our laboratories from basic amino acids for one purpose only.*

Donovan Trueheart was clearly unsatisfied by the reply. A few of the Islanders also began to mutter uneasily amongst themselves; the drones, as the Seti had called them, looked far too human for comfort. Trueheart looked at his supporters knowingly, as if to say: You see? They enslave creatures who look like us! What is to stop them treating us the same way?

We mean you no harm, the Seti continued.

"I don't believe them," Cruse whispered to Kristas.

"Who'd blame them if they did want to harm us?" said Kristas. "We've already killed one of them."

"Will you two shut up!" said Shari. "I can't concentrate with you two bickering."

We have come to offer you all the science of the Seti ... The energy sources and the technology to travel beyond your solar system.

There was an excited babble of interest among Jarrl and the other scientists present. Even Cruse looked intrigued.

Another of the Seti stepped forth; this one spoke in a younger and decidedly feminine voice.

We know that you lack the minerals and resources to travel between star systems, she said. *We offer you that ability.*

Jarrl now stepped forward to join the President. His keen interest showed on his face, but before he could speak, Donovan Trueheart shouted from the crowd: "And what do you want in return?"

The answer which came stunned everyone; but Shari and Kristas noticed that most of all it shocked Jarrl and his fellow scientists.

And Cruse.

We want the Earth.

"Damn them," said Cruse, and Shari saw that he was shaking.

They made a bizarre group, thought Shari as she sat in the Island's main conference chamber. On one side of the table sat the four Seti who had left the ship, and their drones, while on the other sat the President, Shari's father, Donovan Trueheart and several leading scientists and administrators. In one corner of the room stood Quester, leaning on his walking cane and viewing the proceedings with all-knowing saturnine eyes.

Quester had arranged for her and Kristas to be present at this meeting between the humans and the Seti, while Cruse and Kili, along with all the other Islanders had to wait outside. She wondered why, but for some reason Quester seemed to think that it was important that they be present. Like Cruse, Shari began to think that Quester had his own ulterior motives for his actions, and that she and her friends were all being manipulated in some way.

The tallest Seti, who introduced himself as Kriz, addressed the President.

The Seti are a dying race, he explained. *Our home planet has been devastated by solar flares. We are the last of our kind.*

Kriz looked around at the humans, trying to find in their facial expressions an indication of whether they believed him or not. It was vital that they trusted him, otherwise the Seti's entire mission would be a failure.

"And you want to populate the Earth, is that it?" sneered Trueheart. "The world on which Mankind was born, humanity's own Garden of Eden?"

Your former home planet is a burnt-out cinder in space, he pointed out. *You have no further use for it.*

The President and Jarrl exchanged worried looks, which went unnoticed by Trueheart, but not by Kriz.

The Seti however would flourish on Earth, the female Seti went on. *In return we offer you all our technology, the product of over seven thousand years of civilization.*

"And how do we know that you would keep your word?" demanded Jarrl.

You would have to trust us, came the answer. *Without trust no species can ever call itself civilized. The Seti do not lie*, she lied.

We have already instructed our fellow Seti not to leave our ship while these discussions are held, their leader pointed out. *If we meant you harm we could easily have overrun your space station.*

"We only have your word for that," said the President.

Exactly...

The President leaned over to Jarrl and whispered something in his ear. The scientist nodded sadly.

"The Earth – I mean, the Home Planet – is a dead world," she said. "It is not fit for colonization."

The Seti can survive in places where Mankind would die, the female Seti said. *You have already seen how quickly we adapt to your oxygen-rich atmosphere.*

The President glanced once more at Jarrl before continuing. "There are . . . other considerations too." She paused, expecting the Seti to question her further, but they remained silent, staring at her with knowing eyes.

"The Earth is a sacred place," said Trueheart, "the cradle of all humanity." He looked despisingly at the aliens, making no attempt to hide his revulsion at their appearance. "It should not be . . . defiled in such a manner. It is not a home for aliens. You must return from where you came."

We cannot. Our own world has been decimated by solar flares. It is a dead world.

"I am sorry," said the President. "The Home Planet must remain untouched. It is off-limits to Terra-Novans. It must also stay off-limits to the Seti."

Shari looked at Kristas, as if to say: Why? Why must it remain off-limits? What's down there that's so important?

Kriz looked the President straight in the eye: *Then the Seti will die. Do you wish to be responsible for the extinction of an entire species?*

The President stood up. "I'm sorry," she said stonily. "That is not my concern. You will please return to your ship while it is decided what is to become of you."

Suddenly Shari stepped out from where she had been watching the proceedings. There was something about the Seti which fascinated her as much as it did Kristas; perhaps it was their similarity to the dinosaurs she had been so fond of as a child, but she felt that one of the humans ought to stand up for them.

"Why can't they live with us on Mars?" she asked.

"Young lady this is not the time or place!" began the President. "The Seti on TerraNova is clearly out of the question!" she snapped.

"There are whole areas of Mars that haven't been terraformed yet," Shari said, stubbornly calling the planet by its old name. "They could live there."

Jarrl stood up and came over to his daughter. "Not now, Shari," he whispered. "I'll explain later."

Shari gave her father a look of sheer exasperation, but fell silent.

The President addressed the Seti once more: "My guards shall escort you to your ship." She glanced over to a small contingent of leather-clad guards who had been standing discreetly at each of the four corners of the chamber.

"There are other uninhabited worlds in the Solar System," said Jarrl, rather weakly. "Perhaps one of those would be suitable..."

The chief Seti growled, for the first time letting his true feelings show.

Only the Earth is suitable, he said angrily. He rose from his seat and stormed out of the room, followed by his colleagues and the two drones.

Kristas walked up to Shari. "Why won't they listen to them?" he asked. "Why can't we give the Seti a new home? There's nothing left on Earth now!"

Shari didn't reply, just stroked her chin thoughtfully and considered her father. Not only was Jarrl her father, he was also a brilliant scientist, eager for any scrap of new knowledge. The prospect of being given access to all the Seti's technology should, under normal circumstances, have been too much for him to resist.

Yet here he was, doubting the word of the Seti, denying himself the chance to learn the secrets of an entirely new civilization.

It was almost as if he was hiding something.

Reep

"Father, I have to talk to you," Shari called, as she ran after her father who was walking off to his quarters.

Jarrl winced and waited. He wasn't looking forward to this confrontation. The fact that Shari had called him "Father" rather than her more usual "Daddy" didn't bode too well for an easy ride.

He turned to her and smiled weakly. "I was proud of you in the council chamber, you know," he said. "Not everyone would have stood up to Madam President."

Shari shrugged off the praise. "You're hiding something from me, Father, I can tell that."

Jarrl averted his eyes, as his daughter continued:

"Why can't we give the Seti a home? They've done us no harm."

"They wouldn't survive for a year on TerraNova," Jarrl said. "Did you see the look in Trueheart's eyes?"

Shari nodded; there had been hate in the evangelist's eyes, and something else as well.

"He's terrified of them," Jarrl explained. "He's spent the best part of his life spreading his belief that Man is at the very peak of creation, and, with the EarthLifers and his Security staff, has created a considerable power base for himself in the meantime. The Seti could easily destroy all that."

"He's also scared of them because they're different."

"And half of Mankind is scared of them too!" snapped Jarrl. "You've been on TerraNova, Shari, you've felt the unrest in the streets. Half of the people there want to welcome the Seti; the other half want to destroy them, or, at the very best, treat them like specimens in a zoo."

"And which half do you belong to, Father?"

Jarrl didn't answer. "The unrest is threatening to destroy the System completely," he revealed. "People have depended on the System all their life. And now that the Seti have arrived they are going to start questioning its relevance more and more. The Seti have proved that the System isn't quite as all-powerful as it pretends to be."

Shari nodded. It was a flimsy argument but one

which she could, at least, understand, even though she didn't agree with it.

"Then why not Earth?" Shari demanded. This time there was steel in her voice.

"You heard what the President said, the Earth – I mean, the Home Planet – is a dead world."

"No, it's not." There was an awkward silence as father and daughter stared defiantly at each other. Finally Shari continued: "Cruse smuggles people to Earth all the time. He says life there's hard – but at least it's free."

Jarrl looked fondly at his daughter. "You've grown up a lot, Shari," he said.

"I had to," she replied, perhaps more harshly than she had intended. "What's down there that you're not telling me about, Father? What is the System trying to hide from us this time?"

"There's nothing there at all," insisted Jarrl.

"*I don't believe you.* What about this great engineering project everyone seems to be working on, and not talking about?"

Jarrl coloured. "Oh that's nothing important," he said offhandedly. "You'll soon hear of it."

"I want to know now," Shari demanded.

Jarrl took his daughter in his arms, the way he had done when she had been a child. "I lied to you, Shari," he admitted. "There are things down on the Home Planet we should never talk about . . . horrible genetic mutations, more horrible even than the Seti."

Shari looked up wide-eyed into her father's face, as he continued. "In the early years of the last century scientists on TerraNova began a series of top-secret genetic experiments. They were designed to improve homo sapiens, to create a *homo superior*, if you like."

"And the experiments went wrong?"

Jarrl nodded. "The 'results' were sent down to the Home Planet to eke out whatever existence they could. They're still there now."

"But why—"

"People like you, Shari, and Cruse, and the ShantyLanders are starting to question the System," Jarrl reminded her. "If the people were to hear of the genetic experiments all hell would break loose. The System would collapse into anarchy."

"And that's why Earth is off-limits? That's why we can't hand it over to the Seti? To protect the power-sharers in the System?"

"Which would you prefer, Shari?" asked Jarrl. "Order? Or chaos? We all of us have to make that choice at some point in our lives, you know."

Shari pulled herself away from her father's arms. "You've changed, Father," she said, and turned to go.

"I have to see Cruse and Kristas now. I'll see you later, OK?"

Jarrl waved her goodbye. "I might have changed, Shari, but I still love you, you know."

"And I love you too."

Jarrl sadly watched his daughter depart, and then silently congratulated himself. He had told Shari one of the secrets of the System; but it wasn't the real reason the Home Planet was off-limits.

There was another secret down there on the Home Planet: a secret so vast, so important that it would alter Mankind's destiny forever.

It would soon be secret no longer, thought Jarrl. Soon every single soul in the System, from the tree-lined boulevards of TerraNova to the far-flung moons of Saturn, would hear of it, and would marvel, and would rejoice. Now it was only a matter of time.

Jarrl chuckled to himself. *Only a matter of time!* How right he was!

"Jarrl told you that?" Cruse asked in amazement.

After her conversation with her father Shari had gone to the quarters that had been assigned to Cruse. The mercenary looked strangely out of place in his small but luxurious surroundings: Shari had persuaded him to have a shave and a shower, but he still insisted on wearing his grubby black combat outfit, and his boots which were still caked with mud from Avernus.

"Then it's not true?" she asked.

Cruse chuckled. "Oh, it's true enough all right," he said. "There are probably several thousand mutants down on Earth. Of course, there used to be many more..."

"Used to be?" Shari repeated. "Are they dying then?"

Cruse nodded his head wisely. "So he didn't tell you about the cullings then?"

"Cullings?"

"The System doesn't like admitting to its mistakes," he said. "So every so often a detachment from Mars goes down to Earth and slaughters a whole new bunch of mutants."

"But that's horrible!"

"No. It's the System." He stood up from the bed he had been sitting on. "The mutants are *different*, Shari; isn't that what's always happened to people who are different down the ages?"

"But something's got to be done about it," she insisted, suddenly forgetting all about the Seti.

"Maybe something already is being done..." Cruse said meaningfully.

He was turned away from her now so Shari couldn't see his face. If she could have, she would have been surprised at the softness of his usually harsh and hard expression.

"You?" she asked in amazement.

Cruse shrugged, like a naughty little schoolboy, who had suddenly been caught out doing a good deed. Shari suddenly had an urge to rush up to him and give him a hug, but realized that the gesture would not be welcomed.

"They need medical attention, food, arms to protect themselves against their killers," he said. "I provide them with that."

"With the money you take for smuggling people off-world?"

Cruse nodded. "And by taking doctors, scientists to join them. Not everyone wants to be a cog in the System's machinery, you know."

Shari decided to take advantage of Cruse's lowering of his defences to ask him a question she had been wanting to ask for some time now.

"Cruse, why did you agree to take me and Kristas with you? We'd be no help on Earth."

"Maybe you both remind me of myself when I was your age," he said, and there was a touch of regret in his voice, regret for the innocence he had lost when he discovered the truth of the System, and regret too for the brutal slaying of Marla. She would have been proud of what he was doing now.

He turned round, and the hard-faced Cruse was staring at Shari again. "And besides, I needed those ten thousand credits!"

The door slid open and Kristas walked in. There was a look of concern on his face.

"When you weren't in your room I guessed you'd be here, Shari," he said, scowling at Cruse.

"What's wrong, Kristas?" asked Shari.

"It's Doob," he replied. "I've looked everywhere but I can't find her!"

Shari smiled. Doob getting lost seemed so wonderfully normal after the coming of the Seti and what Cruse had just told her. She stood up and walked to the door.

"She's probably poking her nose in places she shouldn't again," she said. "I'll go and look for her. Why don't you stay here, Kristas?" she asked, and smiled at Cruse. "I think Cruse might have something to tell you..."

There was, of course, no day or night as such on the Island, but every seventeen hours or so the interior lights of the Island dimmed to resemble as closely as possible nightfall. In this way the natural body clocks of the Islanders would not be thrown out of sync.

As Shari walked down the long and winding corridors of the space station in search of Doob "night" fell. She found herself walking more carefully, casting a nervous eye behind her every so often. While she knew that all the Seti had returned to their ship she half-expected one of the horrible creatures to leap out of the shadows at her.

She shuddered. How can creatures seemingly so intelligent be so horrific? she asked herself, and then reconsidered. If they look hideous to us, how must we appear to them?

It was a disconcerting thought, and she realized that, like the EarthLifers, she was allowing her gut reactions to get the better of her common sense. The Seti so far had shown no hostility towards the humans, and had meekly accepted their confinement to their craft. Indeed, as she thought more about it there was a strange sort of nobility about the aliens, which even their hideous appearance and stink could not conceal.

Doob was nowhere to be found. Shari tried the recreation rooms, and even the galley of the huge space station but the chimp seemed to have vanished. Finally and with more than a little apprehension she decided to try the docking bay.

The area was in darkness. At the far end of the bay she could see the huge double doors which led to the airlock where the Seti craft was. A shiver of fear ran down her spine, which she instantly dismissed as foolish. There were no guards in the docking bay but she realized that there was no need for them to be there. The double doors were controlled by the Island's central computer, and could not be opened until someone had entered the correct access codes into it. There was no way that the Seti could leave the airlock unless one of the Islanders wished it.

"Doob?" she called out. "Doob, are you here?"

There was a frightened whimpering from behind a bank of instruments. Cautiously, Shari crossed over and looked behind the machinery. In the shadows Doob was cowering, her tiny body shaking all over. Shari picked her chimp up, and cooed softly to her. Still Doob continued trembling.

"What's wrong, Doobie?" Shari asked. "What's frightened you?"

Suddenly Shari heard a scraping noise a few metres away from her. Like the scraping of claws on metal, she realized. She peered into the darkness.

"Who's there?"

No reply.

Putting Doob down, Shari reached for the light control on the wall. The whole docking bay was suddenly bathed in a harsh white light, and Shari drew back and gasped as she saw the intruder's identity.

The young female Seti was standing there, dazed by the sudden light. She hissed, and her long forked tongue flicked over her razor-sharp teeth. Her bloodshot eyes darted this way and that, desperately searching for some means of escape.

It was hard to tell which of them was the more frightened. Certainly Shari was painfully aware that she and Doob were alone with this creature who stood almost seven feet tall and whose muscular arms seemed capable of tearing her to shreds.

Do not be afraid of me, the Seti's voice resounded in her head. It was a distinctly feminine voice.

"I – I'm not afraid," Shari lied, forcing herself to look at the revolting alien creature. The Seti stank of ammonia, and its silvery-white slime trail twisted its way all around the control deck.

"What are you doing here?" Shari demanded more gently.

My people must reach Earth, the creature said. There was a sense of desperation in her voice, and she looked meaningfully over at one of the command consoles set in the wall. The controls on it were covered in slime. Shari realized in an instant what she had been trying to do.

"You won't be able to release your ship from the docking bay by using those controls," Shari said. "You'll have to override the main computer..."

We know little of computer technology, said the Seti. *We rely on the power of the mind and our "technology" is organically grown.*

Shari frowned. The Seti had promised Mankind the use of their technology. But how could people use that technology when it was a kind totally alien to their own?

We could teach you, said the Seti, and, seeing Shari wince, added: *I am sorry. Is it impolite among your people to read the minds of others?*

"Practically impossible," admitted Shari.

Ah, that proves then that the Seti are superior to Man.

Shari felt a tremor run down her spine as the Seti's words provoked in her exactly the same sort of fear they had provoked in Donovan Trueheart and all those who were in favour of destroying the Seti. Shari felt suddenly very inferior – and she didn't like it one little bit.

But you will learn in time – if you will allow the Seti to help you. My name is Reep.

Shari regarded Reep warily as she offered her own name. She glanced over at the airlock doors which were locked. "How did you get in here?" she demanded.

You need not know that, the creature replied.

An awful thought occurred to Shari. The doors could only be opened by someone who had access to the main Island computer: was there a traitor on board?

"Look, just why have you come here?" she asked.

We are a dying race, said Reep. *Our planet is no more and our seed is weak. Soon the Seti too will be no more: millions of years of evolution brought to a final and irrevocable end.*

"I'm sorry." The pain and sadness in Reep's voice was obvious and suddenly Shari saw the Seti creatures in a new and pathetic light.

It is the way of all things, Reep said philosophically. *Our teachers have told us that we must accept death when it comes. And only when one thing ends can another life begin...*

As far as Shari was concerned, Reep was talking in riddles. She picked Doob up once again and cuddled her close; she had about as much chance of understanding her pet chimp as this alien being.

We have travelled for many hundreds of years to come to your planet, Reep said. *Hibernating for most of the time until our instruments alerted us to the fact that we were approaching your Solar System.*

"Hibernating?" asked Shari.

Of course, said Reep. *How else would we have been able to survive the journey?* And then she added meaningfully: *We could hibernate for millions of years if we needed to ... We have come to offer you all the learning of our civilization. And in return we ask only for a place in which to die in peace.*

"But does it have to be Earth?" asked Shari, echoing her father's earlier sentiments. "Surely with your powers of adapting you'd be happy on another planet?"

Reep regarded Shari through cold appraising eyes for long seconds.

The Earth is ... similar ... to the planet on which we evolved. Indeed at one time, so our philosophers tell us, creatures similar to the Seti were masters of your world.

"You mean the dinosaurs?" asked Shari. "Yeah, they survived for — what do you mean 'masters of our world'?"

Suspicion swept over her: were the Seti really as weak as they claimed? Or were they planning on taking over the planet just as the dinosaurs had done all those millions and millions of years ago?

A figure of speech, merely, rasped the Seti. *If the*

dinosaurs had not become extinct when they did, they might now be the creatures terraforming their neighbouring planets and reaching out into space.

"And Mankind wouldn't even get a look in," agreed Shari, and then asked warily: "Look, you're not dinosaurs, are you?" She had noticed the similarities when the Seti had first come aboard.

Reep chuckled. *We share many physical similarities*, she said. *But we followed different evolutionary paths. Many of the dinosaurs on your world were vicious, flesh-eating predators. The Seti are vegetarian and respect all animal life: no race can be as advanced as ours without doing so.*

Shari found herself automatically thinking of the deaths she had encountered since she had left Pasiphae, recalled all the stories people had told about the System executing those who didn't agree with its teachings and laws.

Then she thought about what Cruse had told her of the mutants down on Earth, and how the authorities were systematically slaughtering them.

So far, the Seti had not harmed one single human being, and they had certainly had enough provocation. She raised her eyes to look at Reep once more: was she telling the truth? Did this race of hideously ugly aliens really mean mankind no harm at all? She no longer knew what to think.

"Er, look, I think you'd better go back to your ship,

now," Shari said awkwardly. "Let's just forget this little encounter ever happened, shall we?"

I am grateful, Shari, said Reep and began to move, leaving behind her a trail of foul-smelling slime. *And Shari—*

"Yes?"

Believe me when I say that the Seti mean humanity no harm. Indeed we see in humankind great possibilities, the chance to become the greatest race this Universe has ever known. We respect all life, Shari. We are not interested in death, but survival...

And with those words, Reep walked thoughtfully off towards the airlock leading to her ship. There was much to do, before the Seti could escape from their captivity on the Island and travel down to Earth.

For it was only on Earth that the Seti could complete the glorious and historic mission for the sake of which they had travelled across half a galaxy.

While Shari and Reep were talking, on the main deck of the space station Donovan Trueheart was banging his fists in frustration. The flight deck was in darkness now, attended only by a skeleton crew. When Trueheart had arrived he had dismissed them; as one of the most powerful people in System government his will had to be obeyed.

He had spent long fruitless hours debating the future of the Seti with the President and the space station's scientific elite. The President had suggested that the Seti be allowed to have free access to the Island while their fate was being decided.

Trueheart had exploded at this suggestion, and suggested that the creatures be quarantined. Who knew what virulent space plagues they might have brought with them? he had asked. Didn't the President remember the plagues of the 21st and 22nd centuries which had decimated much of humanity? Far better, he had argued, for the Seti simply to be eliminated, as one would put down an old and tired animal; the Seti ship needn't be destroyed and could then be plundered for its technology.

Finally Jarrl, as a member of the scientific élite, had said that the only thing on which they could all agree was that the Seti should not be allowed on the Home Planet. That, he had said, would be too terrible to contemplate – at least until they knew the Seti better – and could mean the end of almost seventy years of research and planning.

He had then turned to Quester, asking for his support: after all, hadn't Quester been in there at the very start of the project? Quester had smiled and nodded, but said nothing, in that infuriatingly superior manner of his.

The meeting had ended in an impasse, with no conclusion being arrived at, and with Donovan Trueheart storming off to the flight deck where he had dismissed the crew.

The Seti must not be allowed to pose a threat to the

EarthLifers, he decided. Even now, the very mention of their name had caused many of his followers to question his claim that Man was God's chosen creature, destined to carve out his future in the stars. Now that they knew that there was at least one other intelligent race in the Universe, thousands upon thousands of his once-fervent supporters were beginning to doubt his word.

His beady eyes surveyed the battle computer before him; its sequence of flashing lights and LEDs twinkled maliciously at him, taunting him. He smashed his fist on the console again.

His supporters were out there, waiting for his signal that the space station's defence systems had been deactivated and that it was time for them to move in. But what good was their presence when the controls refused to respond to his touch?

He turned as he heard the door behind him open. Kili was standing there, and Trueheart glared evilly at him. Like Cruse, he never liked robots at the best of times but Shari's robot annoyed him even more intensely. He had the feeling that Kili was hiding a lot more than he cared to admit beneath his bumbling exterior.

"What are you doing here, robot?" he snarled.

"I noticed that there was a light on," explained Kili.

"Well, it's not your place to investigate," said Trueheart. "You should have called a security robot if you suspected something was amiss."

"You are quite correct, sir," said Kili. "May I help you?"

"I don't need the help of a walking tin can!"

"I see you have been acquainting yourself with the defence console, sir," Kili remarked. "I am afraid that before it can be operated one must know the correct access codes."

"Do you think I don't know that, robot?" Trueheart asked. "I know one half of the code already..."

"Indeed you do, sir, as is your right as head of System Security," said Kili. "However for the defence console to be fully activated both halves of the code must be entered into the console. And the President has the other half."

"Quite right too," Trueheart harrumped, although it was obvious that he didn't believe that. Then he added, almost as an afterthought: "I don't suppose you know it, do you?"

"Of course not, sir," said Kili. "I am a mere Mark Seven ServoRobot. They don't trust my sort with that type of knowledge."

"And quite rightly so," agreed Trueheart, and marched angrily off the flight deck.

"What a rude little human," Kili murmured to himself as soon as Trueheart had left. "No breeding at all." The robot walked slowly over to the defence console, and punched in a twenty-two digit clearance number onto the computer keyboard. Instantly the entire defence network of the Island was made available to Kili and placed under his sole control.

And then Kili did exactly what Donovan Trueheart had been trying unsuccessfully to do.

He shut down all the space station's defence systems.

The EarthLifers

No one noticed that anything was amiss until several hours later when two young technicians reported for duty on the space station's flight deck. Above the defence console a red light was blazing, indicating that the battle computer had been in use at some time during the night.

Frowning, the technicians discovered that the space station's entire defence systems, apart from those that covered the life-support functions of the Island, had been shut down.

Even that did not concern them unduly; they were, after all, paid not to think, merely to run a daily check on all vital systems on board the Island. Nevertheless, they duly logged in the information, and passed on the news to the offices of the President, Quester and Donovan Trueheart.

The President was still asleep and none of her assistants were willing to wake her: she was known to get particularly tetchy if she didn't get her customary five hours of sleep, and surely the news could wait till then. The attitude of her aides surprised the two technicians, and when they had pressed the matter further, the aides had said that they were under strict orders from Donovan Trueheart not to disturb the President for any reason whatsoever. That surprised them even more but they both knew better than to query the motives of the leader of all System Security, who, in terms of power and influence, was second only to Madam President herself.

Donovan Trueheart, however, never slept, or so it seemed to his acolytes. Once he had learnt of the news he had hurriedly sent them away, before operating the personal communicator which he always carried with him.

He could scarcely believe his luck! Some fool, entrusted with the computer codes, had deactivated the defence systems, and forgotten to reset them! Exactly what he had been trying to do before that blasted robot had interrupted him! He wondered who the person might have been.

For a second he suspected the Seti, but quickly dismissed the notion. The Seti were lumbering hor-rific aliens, he reasoned; they would not be able to comprehend the purpose of the defence controls, let alone operate them.

But who cared who had shut down the Island's defence mechanisms? All that mattered was that they were no longer operational and that, to all intents and purposes, the Island was now defenceless.

Never one to look a gift horse in the mouth, Donovan Trueheart sent out a signal to his fellow EarthLifers, who had been waiting in Martian orbit ever since Trueheart had come on board the Island. Soon they would be here; and soon the threat of the Seti would stop blighting Donovan Trueheart's life forever. And who knows? thought Trueheart, perhaps he could turn the situation even more to his advantage. He remembered the President's stand against him earlier in the conference chamber when she had suggested that the Seti be allowed some sort of free access to the Island while their fate was being decided. She had been standing up to him more and more lately, he had noticed, even though he knew of her secret financial dealing. She was showing too much of a mind of her own, and that was inconvenient to Trueheart's plans. For far too long he had ruled behind the scenes, like the secret service chiefs of ancient Russia in the 20th century; perhaps it was time for Donovan Trueheart to rise to his true and natural station in life.

Exactly three and a half hours after Donovan Trueheart had sent out his signal the President woke up and was immediately informed of the state of the space station's defence systems. Furious that she hadn't been told earlier, she ordered them to be instantly reactivated, and was told a few minutes later that someone – something – had introduced a virus into both the main computer and its back-up. It would take at least two days before the systems could become operational again.

And that was when the President of the System started to get very, very worried indeed.

"What is it?" demanded the President as she, and the rest of the crew, looked at the spacecraft whose image was displayed on the video screen. Its presence so close to the Island had been noticed about an hour ago and now it had finally come into visual range.

The navigator shrugged. "No distinguishable markings, ma'am. And they're not responding to our requests for identification. It could be anyone's..."

"Alien?"

The navigator shrugged again. The President looked despairingly over at Quester.

"Is this anything to do with the Seti?" she asked.

For once even Quester looked worried. He was a meticulous and precise man, who liked to have everything carefully organized and planned: he didn't like the unexpected.

"The Seti ship appears to be of a totally different

technology," he said thoughtfully. "It seems as though it was grown organically, while this intruder is very obviously manufactured. But, as you have instructed, ma'am, I have placed their craft under even tighter security.

"I doubt that they could have anything to do with it, however. If anything I would say it was a Terra-Novan ship. What do you think, Trueheart?"

Donovan Trueheart stroked his chin. "I have never seen such a ship before in my life," he lied, knowing full well that the ship was being piloted by EarthLifers under his orders. "I fear, Your Excellency, that this may be a raider ship."

"Space pirates?" said Shari who, with Cruse and Jarrl, had come onto the bridge when the general alarm had been given.

"There are many valuable minerals and equipment on board this space station," said Trueheart.

"That may be so," said Cruse. "But I've never known pirates to come this close to Mars or Earth before."

"Oh," said Trueheart, making a great display of inspecting his finely manicured nails, "and I suppose that you have a great deal of experience dealing with these criminals?"

"As a matter of fact, yes," came the terse reply. Cruse stared hatefully at Trueheart, remembering Marla.

"Of course it could be something else," continued

Trueheart. All eyes looked to him. "The pro-Seti faction on TerraNova. Perhaps they've come to free their reptile friends?"

The President drew their attention to the screen. The mystery ship was coming closer.

"Whatever it is we're in trouble," she said. "I want an armed guard placed on all the airlocks immediately. Any intruders are to be shot the instant they board the Island."

"That will mean taking guards away from the Seti ship," Quester pointed out.

"Just do it!" she snapped.

As the crew set about their tasks, Shari drew Cruse aside. "Have you seen Kili or Kristas?" she asked.

"No, I thought they were with you," he replied.

Shari shook her head. "I've searched everywhere for them, even before they noticed this ship on the scanners." She was about to say something when the floor beneath her feet shook. Several of the instruments lining the wall of the flight deck burst into flames, and the lights flickered and dimmed.

"What's happening?" she cried anxiously and instinctively clutched Cruse for support.

There was another tremendous *thud!* which seemed to reverberate throughout the entire ship. All around them people were barking out orders, and a warning siren wailed down the corridors of the space station.

"They've docked!" said the President, and operated a communication control on the flight deck before her. "Docking bay two – report!" she barked into the communicator.

"We can't stop them, ma'am," came a frightened voice at the other end of the line. "They've blasted their way through..."

In the background they could all hear the sound of gun fire and people screaming.

"Who are they?" she asked.

"I don't—" Suddenly the line went dead. The President looked up at the others; her face was pale and ashen.

"Gentlemen, I'm afraid we've just been invaded," she said.

Donovan Trueheart's followers, dressed in anonymous brown combat uniforms, were blazing a trail of destruction throughout the Island. The space station's guards were no match for the force of their arms, and the EarthLifers shot down anyone who showed the slightest opposition to them. Relentlessly they made their way to the main docking bay, and the Seti ship.

On the main control deck, as the President co-ordinated the defence of the Island, Donovan Trueheart smiled to himself, satisfied at the success of his plan so far. The other leaders of the System were weak and unfocused, he had decided long ago, and their inevitable dithering and prevarication over the fate of the Seti could put all of humanity at risk.

His EarthLifers, disguised as raiders, would destroy the Seti ship, thereby removing the main threat to Mankind, and, more importantly, the greatest obstacle in his own quest for power. And if the "raiders" should decide to take over the Island in a bloody and terrible coup, and then arrange for the accidental death of the President herself, well, then he could always assume control of the Island, and save the day now, couldn't he?

In all the confusion no one had noticed the missing Kili who had walked onto the flight deck. All eyes were on the video screen and the progress of the raiders, so no one saw him punch out a further series of digits on another control console.

In another part of the space station the great outer doors of the docking bay opened, thereby giving the Seti free access to space again. There had been no alarm given, and the few guards remaining, who had formed a security cordon around the Seti spacecraft, were sucked mercilessly out into space.

Kili sighed to himself; it was a great pity and a tragic waste of human life, he knew; it also went against all the teachings of the Seti. Yet he realized, as did the alien creatures in the egg-shaped craft, and had Quester when he had killed Jared in ShantyLand, that sometimes one evil must be performed so that out of it a greater good can come. And nothing must be allowed to stand in the way of Kili's mission, the mission he had been constructed for over two hundred years ago.

Within the Seti craft there was an enormous feeling of excitement and anticipation as its navigator and pilot prepared to leave the Island. Throughout their long journey, the Seti had rarely allowed their feelings to interfere with their mission. Now several of them felt a rush of unaccustomed joy course through their bodies as they realized their mission was almost at its end.

Their leader cautioned patience. They could not leave quite yet, he reminded them; they still had to wait for their final passengers.

Through the flames and the smoke Kili walked quickly, ignoring the fighting all around him. Taking one final, regretful look at the Island, and with a heavy but stoic heart – if a Mark Seven ServoRobot could be said to possess a heart – he entered the Seti ship.

Amidst all the confusion Shari and Cruse could still feel the shudder as the Seti ship detached itself from the Island. Cruse rushed over to the navigational controls and watched as the egg-shaped craft slowly began its descent down to Earth.

"They must have Kristas on board!" Shari suddenly realized, after she had tried unsuccessfully to call his room once again. "And Kili too! We must rescue them!"

Cruse looked over at Jarrl. "Is there any way we can follow them?" he asked roughly.

Jarrl nodded: he was already leading the way. "There are a couple of skimmers in one of the secondary docking bays," he said. "If you know how to fly them."

Cruse laughed ironically. "I know how to fly them. They're unguarded?"

"Most of the guards are fighting the intruders," said Jarrl. "And besides, these skimmers weren't meant to be in active service at the moment. We were making ... modifications to them."

Cruse raised an interested eyebrow, but chose not to pursue the subject. "Then take us to them!"

As Jarrl hurried on down to the docking bays, Shari asked Cruse: "How do we know where they're going to?"

"Earth of course," he said gruffly. "Where else?"

"But *where* on Earth? Cruse, it's a big planet down there," she pointed out.

Cruse stared at her, with an odd mixture of both approval and annoyance. "You know, Shari, that's about the first sensible thing you've said since I met you ... even I've only seen a small part of it."

"But where are they headed?" she repeated. Cruse shrugged.

"I know," said Jarrl, causing Shari and Cruse to look curiously at him.

"But how could you?" asked Shari.

"They're going to what used to be Central America," he said. Shari and Cruse stared at each other: how did Jarrl know? "The only thing of any worth left on Earth is down there."

They had reached the secondary docking bay. There was no time for any more questions as Cruse hurried them on board the waiting skimmer, and quickly engaged its controls. The skimmer started to slide towards the airlock doors which were slowly opening onto space.

Meanwhile Shari was desperately trying to make connections in her mind, but all she had come up with was a series of baffling and unanswered questions.

Why had the Seti taken Kristas and Kili? Why would they want to make for Central America? What was down there?

And then she remembered something, a half-forgotten fact that she had learnt in her studies at the Academy.

Sixty-five million years ago the dinosaurs, which the Seti resembled so uncannily, had perished. Scientists now accepted that the mighty reptiles' extinction was the direct result of a meteor colliding with the Earth. The dust-cloud from the impact had shut off the heat from the sun for many years, effectively freezing the dinosaurs to death.

The meteor, everyone now agreed, had landed off the coast of Central America.

*

The EarthLifers had cut a bloody and violent course for themselves through the corridors and passageways of the Island. Unused to combat – after all, no one before had even dared to attempt an invasion of the Island – the Island guards could put up little resistance.

Yet Donovan Trueheart's crack security troops, dressed in their space pirate disguises, had been prepared and trained for just such a scenario. They shot down their opponents mercilessly, with no respect at all for their victims' age or sex. Behind them they left a trail of broken bodies, the hapless Islanders who had dared to stand in the way of Trueheart's ambitions.

Silently the EarthLifers made their way to the bridge.

On the bridge the beleaguered President looked beseechingly at Trueheart. The nerve centre of the Island was still secure but on the scanners she could see the fighters she imagined as space pirates making their remorseless approach on the bridge. Her aides on the bridge were no help: to a man they had started to panic.

"Donovan, what can we do?" she asked.

There was a tremor in her normally steady and cool voice. For all her privileged life the President had been guarded and protected; she had never been so close as now to danger and dissent.

Trueheart shook his head, in an affected gesture of despair. "I truly do not know, madam," he said. "I fear that..."

There was an enormous crash and the huge double doors leading onto the bridge burst open, and a horde of EarthLifers streamed into the room, their guns at the ready and their eyes full of murder.

Trueheart smiled a small, almost imperceptible smile, which, however, did not go unnoticed by the President. She looked strangely at Trueheart and then strode forward to address the EarthLifers.

"I am the President of the System," she declared, in the voice which she used at conferences when she wanted to strike terror into her colleagues. "You are in flagrant breach of interplanetary law..."

There was a mocking chuckle from one of the EarthLifers and he turned to his cronies.

"You know something, lads?" he said. "I think she means us!"

The President was nonplussed but continued nevertheless: "And as System President I demand that you lay down your arms!"

There was a further burst of laughter from the EarthLifers, but they did not lower their weapons.

The President had been disobeyed for the first time in her life and she did not know what to do. And then she remembered the person she always used to turn to when one of her System colleagues was showing even the slightest bit of dissent. Donovan Trueheart and his security staff would always come to her aid. Instinctively she looked to Trueheart.

"Donovan, do something!"

Trueheart smiled, and strode forward. He surveyed the EarthLifers before him.

They looked a rough and cruel lot in their space pirate uniforms, and if the truth were to be known Trueheart had nothing but distaste for them. They were content to follow, but never once asked questions or allowed themselves the liberty of one free thought.

Long ago Donovan Trueheart had decided that the human race was divided into masters and slaves, and even though the master that the EarthLifers followed was himself, he still despised them.

However, Trueheart also knew that it would never do for them to know that, and these people he regarded as little more than slaves suited his purpose admirably. He grinned.

"Lay down your arms," he ordered softly.

One by one the EarthLifers lowered their weapons.

The President beamed with pride; she knew that she could trust Donovan, and that her faith in him had never been misplaced. He would be rewarded well for his part in defeating this attack. She came up behind him.

"Well done, Donovan," she began and then frowned.

Trueheart had taken a blaster from one of the "pirates" and was now levelling it directly at her.

"Donovan?" she said nervously. "I don't understand..."

"We've been taken over by 'space pirates', ma'am," Trueheart said. "And I'm afraid that you aren't exactly popular with them."

"Donovan, stop playing this game..."

Trueheart shook his head. "Oh no, ma'am, this is no game. You see, they're rather upset at the monies you embezzle from state funds. Credits which should be going to terraform further parts of TerraNova, and make life easier and the planet more accessible, are going directly into your personal coffers."

"That is nonsense," she claimed but both she and Trueheart knew that it wasn't so. After all, it had been Trueheart who had arranged the whole fraud for her years ago and, in so doing, had guaranteed his influence over her.

"What's more, they've heard disturbing stories about the Home Planet," Trueheart continued. "About genetic experiments that have gone wrong."

"An unfortunate occurrence," said the President. "But that mistake is being remedied. You should know, Donovan – after all, you organized the cullings..."

"And they miss their families and friends too. They'd like the chance for them to travel off-world now and again."

"You know that is impossible. The System is founded on discipline and order, and respect for that order. To have different cultures and colonies mixing is a recipe for anarchy."

"Quite so," said Trueheart, "and I agree with you on all that you say..."

"So put that gun down, Donovan," said the President, "and let us return to getting the Island back into some sort of order."

Trueheart shook his head. "You have ... disagreed with me, Madam President. The Seti are a threat to my power base and must be destroyed, as I demand. And if you will not agree to their extermination then I'm afraid that I will have to carry it out myself."

"Donovan, I expressly forbid you to—"

"You will be forbidding me nothing ever again, Madam President," Trueheart said calmly.

He shot the President full in the stomach. She cried out in agony as the bullets thudded through her body, and she slammed to the floor, dead.

Cowering in the far corner of the bridge were the President's aides. Trueheart looked wearily at them.

"Kill them," he ordered his EarthLifers, and the bridge suddenly exploded with the deafening rat-tat-tat of blaster fire.

When the chamber was silent again Trueheart sighed. "Such a tragedy," he said. "Who would have thought that a renegade band of 'space pirates' could penetrate the System security and assassinate the President herself?''

"I'm sure that the World News Network will say that you put up a spirited and valiant fight in retaking control of the Island, my Lord,'' said one of the EarthLifers, and Trueheart allowed himself the smallest ironic smile.

"I shall be a hero,'' he said. "I must make sure that they say that.''

Then he clapped his hands together determinedly. "And as of now I am Acting System President, and in charge of the Island.'' He turned to the EarthLifers who were already taking over the control consoles on the bridge.

"I want those filthy aliens destroyed now,'' he commanded and then frowned as one of the EarthLifers turned round to him.

"Well, what is it, man!'' he snapped.

"They've gone, my Lord,'' he said, nervously, for fear of invoking his master's wrath. "They're already on their way to the Earth.''

The brow of the Acting System President darkened with rage. "*Damn them!*'' he cried.

The Home Planet

Jarrl looked over at Cruse who was manning the controls of the skimmer.

"Put her into sub-tachyon drive, Cruse," he said. "That's what the Seti will be using to get to the Home Planet."

"This skimmer's equipped with tachyon engines?" he asked incredulously.

Jarrl nodded. "I am a top tachyon engineer and physicist, Cruse," he said. "That's why Quester needed my help in the first place."

"And that's why this skimmer was left unguarded ... the modifications you talked about."

Cruse looked suspiciously at Shari's father and then nodded, and activated the necessary controls; if they were lucky the extra speed that gave them might help them catch up with the Seti before they reached Earth.

"The Seti know about tachyons too, huh?" he asked.

"How else would they have been able to cross all those light years of space?" said Jarrl, then added meaningfully, "But perhaps they don't know as much as we do..."

"You were one of the pioneers in tachyon research, weren't you, Father?" asked Shari.

"One amongst many, Shari," he admitted.

"But I don't understand why they're so important," she said.

"Tachyons are sub-atomic particles which travel faster than light," he began.

At the control desk Cruse grunted. "Even I know that," he said.

"If we were able to harness fully the power of the tachyon can you imagine the possibilities that would open up to us?" Jarrl asked.

"To travel faster than light?" shrugged Shari.

"The closest star to Earth is Proxima Centauri," said Jarrl. "It's a little over four light years away from us."

"That's twenty-four million million miles to you and me, Shari," Cruse said casually. "Even if we could travel at the speed of light it'd take us four and a half years to reach it."

Jarrl looked up curiously at Cruse. "I wouldn't have thought that you would have known that," he said.

"I studied physics under you at the Academy," he reminded him, as he adjusted the controls of the skimmer. Even now the rusty-brown globe of Earth was coming into view. There was still no sign of the Seti's ship.

"I don't remember you," said Jarrl.

"No, I don't suppose you would," Cruse replied. "You probably had more important things on your mind."

Jarrl glared at Cruse.

"But what have tachyons to do with the Seti – and Central America?" asked Shari.

"Yes, Jarrl Sharifi, you tell us," goaded Cruse.

Shari had the strangest feeling that Cruse, who had journeyed to Earth many times in the past, already knew half of what Jarrl was about to tell them.

Jarrl took a deep breath. "The System has been trying to harness fully the power of the tachyon for the past nine years," he began.

Since you left me, thought Shari.

"If we could just create a tachyon drive – and not just an inferior sub-tachyon drive – we'd be able to provide ourselves with an immeasurable power source," said Jarrl. Neither Cruse nor Shari could mistake the enthusiasm in his voice.

"Think of it, Shari: journeys which, under the conventional laws of physics, would take years, or even decades, we could accomplish in mere days! Even now, centuries after Neil Armstrong first set foot upon the Moon, we can only travel within our own Solar System. With full tachyon power we'd be able finally to break out amongst the stars! Mankind could finally fulfil its destiny!''

Shari shuddered. Her own father was beginning to sound like an EarthLifer; was the scientist's quest for knowledge so all-consuming? She remembered his acceptance of the mutants down on Earth; Jarrl might once have been an unwilling participant in the System's schemes, but now it seemed that even he had been tainted with its amoral sense of values.

She considered the matter. There was no doubt that what her father was saying was true. For far too long now Mankind had been in a technological cul-de-sac. Pluto, the outermost planet of the solar system, had proved to be the limit for Mankind's spacecraft. But with full tachyon power ... well, the results would be incalculable! It could be the most important discovery for Mankind since the invention of the wheel.

''We'll be entering Earth atmosphere within the hour,'' said Cruse.

Already the image of the Earth filled the screen. Shari looked at it in wonder: Earth, the home planet of humanity! What was there for the Seti?

''What's down there, Father?'' She pressed home the question once more.

Jarrl hesitated, as if weighing up the consequences of letting his daughter and Cruse in on the secret which had occupied TerraNova's scientific elite for the past decade.

Cruse looked over to him, "I think it's about time your daughter and I were told the truth, Jarrl," he said. "I've heard the rumours about a massive engineering project on Earth, even though I've never seen it. But then I've never been to Mexico either."

Finally Jarrl reached his decision.

"The Tachyon Generator," he said. "The means to produce as much tachyon energy as possible. With such a power source we'd at last be able to leave the Solar System behind. It would be the start of the Great Break Out, when we finally have the energy reserves and the capability to travel out to the stars."

Shari was almost overwhelmed by the quasi-religious fervour with which Jarrl discussed the Tachyon Generator. A few days ago she had never left her home world of Pasiphae, and yet now here she was discussing with her own father the best way to travel between the stars!

"And you think the Seti want to steal this energy from us?" she asked.

Jarrl nodded, but Shari wasn't quite convinced. She remembered her meeting with Reep in the docking bay: Reep had said that her people meant no harm to Mankind. For some reason Shari still believed her.

"Although who knows what use they'll put it to?"

Jarrl said. "Their technology is so different from ours after all. If they combined the two technologies in some way…"

Cruse turned round in his seat. "It looks like you're right, Jarrl," he said, and indicated a screen on the navigational panel which was tracking the flight path of the Seti's ship. "They're coming in to land in Central America – right where you said they would!"

He pointed to another set of co-ordinates on the screen. "And we've got company too. A ship from the Island is right on our tail!"

"This is the Acting President of TerraNova. Give yourself up, aliens," Donovan Trueheart's voice crackled over the radio waves, and was picked up by Cruse's ship too. "Or we blast you off the face of the planet."

Cruse, Jarrl and Shari looked despairingly at each other, as they manoeuvred their skimmer into a flight pattern ready for planetfall. The Seti ship had just landed on the planet's surface.

"Can they do that?" Shari asked nervously.

Cruse checked the navigational controls which both recorded the flight path of Trueheart's craft, and also its design. He nodded.

"The Island's defences are down but his own ship will still be armed. And if he does fire – well, we're right in the way."

You will not fire, Donovan Trueheart, the voice of

the Seti was heard to say over the communication network. It was calm and self-assured. *We have Kristas, one of your fellow humans, on board.*

"Kristas!" gasped Shari. "We were right – they've taken him as hostage. They can't attack the ship while Kristas is on board."

Jarrl put an arm around his daughter's shoulder. "Don't be so sure, Shari," he said. "You heard what Trueheart called himself – the 'Acting President'. Those raiders were EarthLifers, and he's just staged himself a coup. He'll stop at nothing to strengthen his power base."

Sure enough, a moment later they heard Trueheart declare: "The young boy is nothing – a necessary sacrifice to ensure the continued survival of the human race!"

Shari looked aghast. "We have to do something!" she said, and then stopped as she heard the Seti's reply.

Perhaps the human race is not fit for survival, it said, *if you are willing to dispose so easily of another's life, Acting President Trueheart . . . Perhaps only the Seti are fit to live.*

"What are they saying?" asked Shari, and turned to her father. "Are they going to destroy us?"

"They said they were a dying race," said Jarrl. "Do they mean to take us with them?"

And yet you will not fire on us, continued the Seti.

Destroy the Seti and you also destroy the Tachyon Generator.

"Of course!" said Jarrl. "They're calling Trueheart's bluff! They've landed in the very centre of the Generator complex. If he fires on their ship he'll also hit the Generator! It took decades of research and nine years' hard labour to build it; Trueheart won't sacrifice that."

Shari wasn't entirely convinced; she was sure that Trueheart would risk everything in his quest to rid the System of the aliens.

"What if he does decide to open fire?" she asked her father. "What if he does hit the Generator?"

Jarrl's face turned ashen but he didn't reply. Shari looked to Cruse for an answer.

"The biggest bang in history," he said darkly.

"At least the Home Planet is uninhabited," said Jarrl, as Cruse and Shari looked worriedly at each other.

"You know it's not, Jarrl," said Cruse coldly.

"Oh? The mutants, you mean?" Jarrl said, embarrassed at his *faux-pas*. "Yes, I was forgetting about them…"

Shari regarded her father with disbelief. Did the shattered results of Mankind's bio-experiments mean so little to him then that he could conveniently forget about their existence? Could the System corrupt so much even the kind man she had known as her father?

If the Tachyon Generator was destroyed by either Trueheart or the Seti then the mutants on the planet, whom Cruse had protected as far as possible from the cullers of the System would also be destroyed, charred to a crisp in a nanosecond.

"We're coming in to land," announced Cruse as the skimmer entered the Earth's atmosphere.

"And then what do we do?" asked Shari gloomily.

"Ah," said Cruse. "I was rather hoping that you were going to tell me that."

The Tachyon Generator was a gigantic power plant, the size of a small city. Over an area of almost twenty square kilometres, huge parondite pipes stretched, carrying the valuable minerals mined on Jupiter to the nine hundred and fifty-one reactors which provided the power for the Tachyon Generator.

Along the metal walkways there was not a trace of any human habitation. Instead, mindless robotic drones cruised along the walkways, fulfilling the tasks that they had been programmed to do almost a decade before. It was only rarely that a group of TerraNovan scientists came down to the plant to check up on the running of the Generator; most of the running of the project was conducted by the drones.

They were incapable, too, of defending any part of the Generator against alien intrusion; after all, there was no need, as the Generator was protected constantly by the watchful eye of the Island up in space, and the mutants who had been despatched to Earth by the System had, for the most part, been sent to the northern hemisphere of the planet. The drones' creators had reckoned, of course, without Kili's closing down of all their defence systems, and now the Generator was unprotected and supremely vulnerable.

At the very centre of the complex was a huge semi-circular arena, almost as large as the crater on Pasiphae in which Shari and Kristas had first met Cruse and the ShantyLanders. A man standing at the centre would have been unable to see the rim of the arena, almost a kilometre away.

If he had been able to see that far, however, he would have seen that the arena was surrounded by a series of gigantic latticed screens, which towered up into the sky; banks of controls lay at the foot of the screens.

The arena was open to the sky, and it was here that the Seti ship had landed, close to one of the screens. There was no sign of the Seti, or Kristas and Kili.

A heavy mist hung over the place as Cruse's skimmer touched down, after having completed a brief reconnaissance scan of the area. In response to Shari's question, Jarrl explained that the mists were probably some chemical by-products of the tachyon generation process, but reassured her that they were not poisonous – at least not to humans.

As they left the skimmer Shari pointed out to him

the dead soil on which they were standing: she doubted that anything would ever be able to grow here again. Was this also the by-product of Man's researches into tachyon technology?

Jarrl shrugged: there was always a price to pay for progress, he said.

Shari stared at her father in disbelief. She remembered her visits to St Paul's Cathedral and the Taj Mahal in Virtual Reality; their beauty too had been destroyed in the name of progress by the System. Did the System destroy everything it touched – even her own father? She was about to say something, but Cruse shook his head sadly.

Ignoring Shari's indignation, Cruse pointed up into the sky. Trueheart's ship was visible now and was coming in to land some way from them. From out of his side holster he pulled the gun he had taken when the EarthLifers had boarded the Island.

As they approached the banks of controls and instruments at the foot of the latticed screens, they could hardly believe their eyes. The place was crawling with Seti; they had assumed that the Seti ship, large as it was, had only carried a handful of the creatures, but here there were hundreds of them.

Most of them were hunched over the control panels, oblivious to the presence of the approaching humans. The three-fingered claws had difficulty manipulating the controls which were originally designed for creatures with five fingers on each hand,

and every so often they were obliged to call on the services of one of their Neanderthal-like drone servants.

Shari winced. The Seti's drones looked so much like human beings, and it was hard to believe that the Seti had grown them in their laboratories. She supposed that they had no feelings and little intelligence, and yet it was still difficult to remain comfortable when she saw the Seti treat them as little more than senseless beasts of burden, as she might treat the little robotic Earth drones who buzzed around the project, their pre-programmed and unthinking brains uncomprehending of what was happening around them.

The Seti still hadn't noticed them, and Shari turned to her father. "What are they doing?" she asked.

"Whatever it is it's vitally important to them all," he said.

"You must know," hissed Cruse. "You were partly responsible for building this thing."

"The Generator was intended to produce a ready source of tachyon energy," Jarrl said. "But the adjustments they're making to it are making no sense to me at all..."

Cruse stared at him, and then shook his head despairingly. "What you really mean is that the Seti know more about this blasted project than you scientists do yourselves!" Jarrl's silence was answer enough.

Shari searched the crowd of gathered Seti for any sign of Kristas; the young man was nowhere to be seen. She guessed he must still be in the Seti ship and was about to suggest to Cruse that they steal away into the egg-shaped craft when, standing in the midst of the Seti, she saw—

"Kili!" she called out happily.

Despite Cruse's efforts to hold her back, she began to run towards the seven-foot robot. Alerted by her call, Kili turned around: he saw Shari racing towards him, followed closely by Jarrl, and Cruse, carrying his gun.

Suddenly Shari froze dead in her tracks. Kili was pointing a gun at them, a gun far larger and obviously much more deadly than Cruse's.

Cruse and Jarrl skidded to a halt by Shari. "Damn robot," Cruse cursed. "He's just like the one who stood by and let Marla be killed. I knew we couldn't trust him."

Jarrl shook his head, genuinely unable to understand what was happening. "Kili's a ServoRobot," he said. "He's not programmed for defensive capabilities."

"Don't you bet on it," growled Cruse.

Kili continued to point the blaster at Shari's group while behind him the Seti and their drones continued with their work, seemingly unconcerned by the humans' presence.

"Greetings, Shari," Kili said, and Shari frowned: was there a touch of sadness in her old friend's voice.

"Kili? I don't understand," she said, and stepped forward.

"Please do not make me use this gun, Shari," Kili said.

"What do you mean?"

"If you come any closer I shall have to kill you, I'm afraid. Nothing must be allowed to interfere with the Seti's great mission."

"I knew it!" said Cruse. "He's been in league with the Seti all along."

Shari shook her head, scarcely able to take it all in. Tears of disappointment and betrayal streamed down her face as she remembered all the curious little instances of Kili knowing more than he should, of his being capable of much more than a mere Mark Seven ServoRobot should have been.

She recalled that he had shown no surprise when she and Kristas had first mentioned the Seti; was it possible that he had been a double agent for the aliens all this time? But, if so, how had they contacted him from out of space? And why was he helping them now?

"It can't be," Shari sobbed. "He's my friend."

"Remember you told me that he had helped to bring up Jarrl," Cruse said. "He was probably the one who got him interested in tachyons in the first place... And you never could tell me exactly where the blasted tin can came from."

Jarrl knew the pain that Shari must be going through; as Cruse had said, Kili had helped to bring him up as well as his daughter. He looked curiously at his old friend.

"You know you cannot kill us, Kili," he said firmly. "You're a ServoRobot: your prime directive is not to harm humans. You're physically incapable of hurting us."

In answer Kili fired a bolt of energy at the scientist's feet. Jarrl leapt back in horror.

"But... but how...?" he stammered.

"When I was constructed over two hundred years ago I was indeed built with that prime directive," Kili explained. "Since then I have been ... deprogrammed.

"It was all part of the Seti's great plan," he continued.

"But how?" asked Shari, through her sobs. "You were made on Earth. How could you be part of their plans? They've never been to Earth before ... or have they?"

"As of this moment in time the Seti have never set foot on Earth before," Kili said mysteriously, and Shari wondered at the robot's odd turn of phrase.

As of this moment in time. What did he mean?

And then she remembered another similar phrase

she had once heard him using: *Only a matter of time, Shari, everything is only a matter of time...*

She was aware of Kili pausing for a moment, as if weighing up whether to tell her anything else. She was also painfully aware that he still kept his gun firmly trained on all three of them.

"The Seti had ... *have* ... an agent," Kili said.

"But who?"

Kili would not reply, but, by Shari's side, Cruse nodded his head wisely.

Quester, he thought. He was sure of it: Quester had been manipulating things all along. Shari had told him about Jarrl's unwelcome guest of nine years ago who had recruited him for the tachyon project.

And without Jarrl's expertise, Cruse realized, the Tachyon Generator would never have been completed in time for the Seti's arrival.

It had been Quester who had vetoed Kristas's posting to the Island at the hearing of the Board, and probably the one who had arranged a dead-end job for Shari. He had known all along that their frustrations would make them want to leave their home world, not as employees of the System, but as rebels and runaways. He had set into action the whole series of events which had led them here.

He had also provided them with the transponder codes which had enabled them to get to the Island.

And once on the Island Kili had been able to free

the Seti's craft so that the aliens could travel on down to the Earth and the Generator.

And suddenly, Cruse realized that Quester hadn't been particularly interested in getting Shari and Kristas and himself to Earth. Quester had indeed saved them when they escaped from the detention centre, but that was only because he needed Shari alive to ensure Jarrl's continued co-operation.

It was Kili that Quester had been interested in all along, a ServoRobot who, like every other Servo-Robot, was not allowed to travel off-world. Quester wasn't willing to risk his own skin, and detection by Trueheart, and arrange for Kili's transportation himself. And so what better way than to have the robot brought to Earth by three rebels, three rebels who had foolishly played right into the wily old man's hands?

And yet...

The Seti had never been on Earth or Mars before. How could they have recruited Quester to their cause? He knew that the aliens were telepathic, but surely they weren't so powerful that their thoughts could cross the thousands of light years to Earth?

"How could you, Kili?" sobbed Shari. "How could you go and betray us like this?"

He is not betraying you, Shari. Reep, the Seti Shari had met on the Island, had left her colleagues and come to join them.

"Reep? What do you mean?" Cruse and Jarrl stared at Shari, wondering how the two knew each other.

"You lied to me," said Shari. "You said that you were concerned for the future of Mankind..."

She gestured at the latticed screens of the mighty Tachyon Generator. "And what are you doing here? Planning its destruction?"

Reep shook her head violently. *I told you, even as our race nears its natural extinction we still value all life. The Seti are concerned about the future of humanity,* she claimed. *And also about its past.*

Shari stared at her erstwhile friend in blank incomprehension, but Jarrl seemed to have an inkling of what the female Seti was talking about.

"Tachyons travel faster than light ..." he began.

That is correct.

"So with the right technology they would allow you to travel through time."

"But I don't understand," said Shari. "Why do you want to travel through time?"

Think of the dinosaurs, Shari, was the enigmatic reply.

"The dinosaurs?" Shari didn't understand.

She was about to press Reep on the matter, when a mighty blast of plasma energy shot past her and hit Reep full in the chest. Part of the Seti's chest exploded in a shower of blood, and she thudded to the floor.

"Get down!" Donovan Trueheart roared at Shari, Cruse and Jarrl as his EarthLifer troops streamed into the arena, their guns blazing.

The Seti looked up, strangely calm, and then

returned to their work. The EarthLifers started to fire on them, but the aliens offered no resistance. One by one they fell to the ground, as Trueheart's troops mowed them down.

Shari, who had flung herself to the ground, watched on in horror. The Seti drones were shrieking in terror and scattering, but the Seti seemed strangely unperturbed by all the chaos and carnage around them. They continued to operate the controls of the Tachyon Generator as, all about them, their colleagues fell.

Shari suddenly realized that the Seti were obsessed, as obsessed as her father had become by his great god of science, or as Trueheart was in his quest for power.

Only Kili came to the Seti's defence, shooting down the EarthLifers with his blaster, but he was only one against the scores of troops Donovan Trueheart had brought with him down to Earth.

Yet the sight of her trusted and normally placid Kili viciously shooting humans down dead horrified Shari even more than the mass slaughter of the Seti; she suddenly realized, with a shudder, just why Cruse had always been uneasy in the robot's presence.

"Destroy the aliens!" bellowed Trueheart, who was watching, wild-eyed, from a distance. "The System must remain pure!"

Cruse, who had taken cover behind a bank of machinery as soon as the shooting had begun, fingered his own gun uncertainly. Trueheart's bloodlust and hate of the aliens was disturbing even to him, as, for the first time in his life, he found he wasn't sure in which direction to fire.

Some of the EarthLifers' shots were going astray, hitting the control panels of the Tachyon Generator, and causing several of them to burst into flame. It was only then that the few remaining Seti showed any sign of concern or excitement. They snarled angrily at the humans, and then continued with their work. The air was filled with the stench of acrid smoke and the burning rubber of the cables which connected the control consoles to the tachyon generators.

Shari had managed to crawl over to the prone figure of Reep. Thick and sticky blood was pouring out of the Seti's chest wound, and her breath was coming sharp and short.

"Reep . . ." Shari said. "Are you all right?"

I am dying, Shari. . . .

"There must be something we can do?"

There is nothing. Reep's voice was strangely calm. *Our task here is nearly over . . . Soon our dying race will be no more.*

Shari gestured over to the EarthLifers. "I'm sorry . . . We didn't bring them."

I know. Reep turned to look at Shari. *What a sad and frightened race you humans are . . . divided into factions, always squabbling amongst yourselves . . . And yet with so much potential, so much promise.*

That is why we came here, Shari. The Seti are dying, but before we die we must ensure that that promise comes to fruition.

"I still don't understand."

The dinosaurs, Shari, remember the dinosaurs, Reep said once more and then died.

The shooting had stopped, and a ghostly silence hung over the area. All but a handful of the Seti had been slaughtered by Trueheart's men, and now the EarthLifers were surrounding the surviving aliens. No one noticed Shari who slipped quietly away and headed towards the Seti's craft.

Trueheart stepped forward and gazed hatefully at the aliens and Kili, who had lowered his blaster. He indicated the latticed screens which towered above them: they were glowing.

"What have you done?" he demanded.

We have activated the Tachyon Generator, said Kriz.

Trueheart glanced at Jarrl for confirmation of the fact.

"That's impossible, Lord Trueheart," Jarrl said. "The project isn't complete yet."

We have allied our own technology with that of Earth, said Kriz.

Jarrl looked at Kili. "Is this true?" he demanded.

Kili confirmed that it was. "The controls are locked, you cannot reverse what the Seti have done," he said, and then added almost as an afterthought:

"The Generator is also primed to self-destruct in – oh, I'd say about thirty minutes' time."

Shari approached the Seti ship warily, worried lest any of the Seti had remained behind to guard it. Her worries were unfounded, however, for the ship was empty, its winding corridors dark and eerily silent. Sitting outside the egg-shaped craft were Kristas and Quester, who had travelled in the Seti ship with him and Kili.

Shari rushed up to her friend. "Kristas, are you all right?"

Kristas shrugged off her concern.

"I thought they'd kidnapped you," she said. He smiled.

"Well, they did, sort of," he said. "Kili said they needed me as a hostage so that Trueheart wouldn't attack them."

Shari sneered. "Well, that didn't work out then, did it?"

"No ..." he said. "I got the feeling that they were genuinely shocked when they discovered that my life meant nothing to him."

"To the Seti all life is sacred," said Quester. "That is what will make their task even harder for them."

Shari frowned. "What task?"

Quester smiled enigmatically. "Kristas will tell you," he said, and stood up, supporting himself on his walking cane. "And now I must go. I have a long journey ahead of me."

Kristas looked at the departing figure of the old man. "A journey of sixty-five million years maybe?" he asked.

"Something like that," said Quester. "The Seti will need help in their unfamiliar new world, help from someone who knows that world. I'm an old man now, and there is no future for me in the System, knowing what I do. So before I die I'd like to help the Seti one final time in their great task." He turned and disappeared into the Seti ship.

"Kristas, what is going on?" asked Shari.

"Kili and the Seti told me everything," he said. "I understand now – they're on our side after all."

"Kili told you everything about what?" Shari demanded, irritated now.

There was a knowing twinkle in Kristas's eyes. "You're really going to like this one," he said. "The dinosaurs, Shari, it's all to do with the dinosaurs."

The latticed screens were glowing white-hot now as the Tachyon Generator, allied with the Seti's alien technology, reached full power. When Kili had announced the imminent destruction of the Generator Trueheart and his troops had retreated to their ship, abandoning the Seti in their panic.

"I would also leave if I were you," Kili advised Cruse and Jarrl who had been left behind.

"Shari! Where's Shari!" cried Jarrl, noticing his daughter's absence for the first time. Cruse pointed over to the Seti ship; Shari and Kristas were running towards them.

"Cruse," she panted when she had reached them. "The Seti ... they must be allowed to leave..."

"Who cares about them now?" Cruse said angrily. "This place is going to go up in flames any second now."

Jarrl looked wildly about. The skimmer which had brought them to Earth was too far away: they would never reach it in time.

"Follow me," Cruse said and led them away from the Generator. "There are some bunkers near here. I saw them when I did the reconnaissance when we arrived here."

"Bunkers?" asked Shari.

"Remember I told you?" he said. "From the wars a couple of centuries ago? That's the only place we're going to be safe now."

Kristas and Jarrl raced after Cruse, but before Shari followed them she turned to Kili.

"Kili, Kristas told me," she said. "I understand everything now."

"I am glad."

"You're going with them?" she asked, although she already knew the answer.

"They will need my assistance," he said. "It will be a wild and untamed world sixty-five million years ago. That is why Quester built me over two hundred years ago, for just this purpose. And that is why he allowed you and Kristas to come to Earth."

Shari and Kristas exchanged amazed looks.

"Think about it, Shari," Kili said. "A robot travelling alone to Earth? Robots aren't allowed off-world without their human masters. You provided me with my alibi. The Seti are supreme pacifists – they will need my protection in the new world which awaits them." He paused and then said: "I know it is illogical, but I will miss you, Shari."

Shari nodded. "I'll miss you too, Kili," she sniffed, and then raced after the others.

Ten minutes later the Tachyon Generator, the crowning achievement of TerraNovan science, exploded in a massive unchecked outburst of energies. The conflagration was visible to Donovan Trueheart and the EarthLifers as they orbited the Earth in their ship, and the explosion rocked the underground bunker in which Shari, Kristas, Cruse and Jarrl had taken shelter.

Hours later, when the EarthLifers touched down once more on the planet, and when Shari and her friends had emerged from their bunker, the Tachyon Generator was little more than a smoking ruin.

Of Kili, the Seti, and their ship there was no sign.

EPILOGUE

S hari looked down affectionately at the Mexico Stone, that mysterious chunk of rock which had confounded scientists for so long. Experts had debated for a long time just how a streak of an alloy, manufactured only about two hundred years ago, could have found its way into the centre of a stone sixty-five million years old. Shari and Kristas now knew the answer.

"So long, Kili," Shari whispered, and took a final look at the last remaining vestige of the robot who had brought her up.

Who would have thought that a Mark Seven ServoRobot, constructed only two hundred years ago, would end up sixty-five million years in the past?

She turned away from the stone and wandered into

the adjacent dinosaur hall. Kristas was standing there, gazing up at the reconstructed skeleton of the Tyrannosaurus rex with a new-found interest.

"It's marvellous, isn't it?" he said.

"I'm glad you finally agree!"

"To think that if the dinosaurs had survived they'd have been the dominant form of life on Earth," he said.

"And poor old humans like us wouldn't have got a look in," Shari agreed. "But the Seti saw us right, didn't they? Travelling back in time and destroying the dinosaurs."

"How do you think they did it?" Kristas asked. "Quester wouldn't tell me."

Shari shrugged. "Sent Kili on a hunting expedition?" she said flippantly and laughed at the thought of the robot fighting off the mighty killer reptiles of Earth's prehistory. "He'd probably run at the sight of the first Brontosaurus!" She remembered what she had learnt at the Academy: "We've always supposed that Earth collided with a meteorite, and that the explosion created a dust storm which shut out the sun's light."

"So?"

"Well, meteorites aren't the only things which can explode, are they?"

"They blew up their own spaceship?"

"Maybe."

"Then it was suicide," breathed Kristas sadly.

"No," said Shari firmly. "Reep told us the Seti were

dying anyway. But they saw a chance to create a new life, to bring Mankind into the world, and they took it."

"Like an interplanetary midwife."

Shari smiled. "If you like ... but what does it matter? The Seti destroyed the dinosaurs, but not before they put one of their members into hibernation on Earth. Reep told me that they could hibernate for millions of years if they had to."

"Until he woke up sixty-five million years later, where he met Quester as a young boy. Before he died he told Quester everything, and Quester built and programmed Kili in time for their arrival," finished Kristas.

"But there's one thing I don't understand," said Shari. "The Seti's home planet is thousands of light years away from us. How did they know so much about us? How did they know about the dinosaurs?"

"Simple," said Kristas. "Radio waves. When our Seti arrived in the past they sent a message to their home planet..."

"Telling them of the threat the dinosaurs posed to us," Shari realized. "Telling them that when their own race was dying they should come to Earth to save *our* race."

"The Seti thought of everything."

"We're on our own now, though," said Shari. "The Seti believed humanity was worth saving. Now we've got to prove ourselves worthy of their faith in us."

She heard someone call her name and turned around to see Jarrl approaching them. She rushed up to him.

"Father, what have they decided?" she asked anxiously.

"A computer error ..." he said awkwardly.

"*What*?"

"The destruction of the Tachyon Generator," he explained. "Too much energy was channelled into the Generator because of a programming error and it exploded."

"But the Seti—"

Jarrl shrugged. "The Seti? A huge hoax according to the World News Network," he said. "President Trueheart has promised that he'll bring those responsible for the deception to justice."

"*President* Trueheart?" said Kristas, scarcely able to believe what he was hearing.

"The System praised his efforts in fighting off the space pirates who boarded the Island," said Jarrl, and added: "It was a unanimous decision."

"But the pirates were his own EarthLifers! He organized the coup against the President himself!" protested Shari. "You know that as well as we do!"

"Keep your voice down, Shari," said Jarrl. "You don't know who might be listening ... It's the System, Shari."

"No, it's a lie."

"What do you think would happen if people knew

the truth?" asked Jarrl. "To know that we owe our existence to a race of aliens? To know that even the theory of evolution has been called into question?"

Shari was intrigued. "What do you mean?"

"The Seti's drones," said Jarrl. "You saw how much like us they were. Imagine what some people are saying already."

"That we're their descendants?" asked Kristas.

Jarrl didn't answer.

"The System's changed you, Father," Shari said coldly. "When I knew you you were a kind man ... and then you left me."

"The System was threatening your life," he protested, and looked warily about him. No one was watching them or listening to them.

"I know ..." she said slowly. "But over the years you've changed. You've become a part of the System – well-meaning maybe, but as callous and as cold as everyone else who works for it."

"We must all of us survive, Shari," Jarrl said. "Do you think that I'm entirely happy with the way the System works? With the treachery and deceit? With the mutants down on Home Planet..."

"It's nice that you've remembered them," she said sarcastically. "Cruse told me you'd conveniently forgotten about them again."

Jarrl ignored the comment. "We have to accept the System, Shari," he pleaded. "Survive in it the best way we can ... and I'm a member of the scientific elite. That gives me certain privileges, certain protections. And it gives you, as my daughter, the same protections and privileges. You can't fight the System, Shari, you must realize that. That's what being an adult is all about."

Shari remained silent.

"So what happens to us?" asked Kristas.

Jarrl brightened, glad to be able to give them some good news at last.

"There will be no charges brought against you two, of course, or your friend Cruse, in view of your 'sensitive' knowledge – and the fact that you're my daughter, Shari," he added pointedly.

"Well, thank you very much," Shari said under her breath.

"In fact, you've both been given clearance to live on TerraNova," he continued. "The System and the Board back on Pasiphae have noted your interest in ancient Earth history, Shari. There's a vacancy coming up as curator of the science museum soon; they think you'd be the ideal person to fill it. And there's a great deal of work to be done on some of the 23rd century war documents in the book room: they're wondering whether Kristas would be interested in translating them. After all, we really ought to find out why Brazil and China bombed each other out of existence all those years ago, oughtn't we?"

"So we can both become happy and contented members of the System, is that right, Father?"

"Yes. So what do you both say? Isn't that great news?"

He wondered why neither of them was smiling.

Cruse smiled.

He tried to offer his hand for them to shake but that would have meant dropping Doob who was chittering merrily in his arms. Ever since they had returned to the Island and then TerraNova, the mercenary and Shari's pet chimp had been inseparable.

"I got your message," Cruse said. In fact he had been waiting for days now for Shari and Kristas to contact him, and ask him to meet them in their quarters in New Canberra. "Are you sure you still want to go through with this?"

Shari and Kristas looked at each other and nodded: they'd never been more sure of anything in their lives.

"The System isn't for us," said Kristas. "Just as it wasn't for you."

"We came prepared this time," said Shari, and indicated the backpacks that each of them carried over their shoulders. They were bulging with food packs and nutrition bars.

"And just where are you thinking of going?" asked Cruse.

"The Earth first perhaps," said Shari. "We never did get to meet the people you help down there."

Cruse grunted approvingly. "And then?"

"It's a big Universe, Cruse," said Kristas. "We and the Seti can't be the only ones out there."

"Will you help us again?" asked Shari. "We'd understand it if you didn't. After all, the System is prepared to forget any offences you might have committed in the past—" she looked him in the eye and added slyly "in return for your silence."

"And you really believe that?" asked Cruse. "A few months and I'm sure there'll be a convenient 'accident' which gets us all out of the way. Remember I saw Donovan Trueheart kill Marla and the others all those years ago. We're a threat to him: we know too much. He'll stop at nothing to maintain his power base."

"You haven't given us an answer," said Shari.

Cruse sniggered. He realized that Shari and Kristas already knew what his answer would be.

"Do you have a ship?" asked Kristas, surprising himself by being practical for once.

"The latest technology," Cruse said. "Sub-tachyon drive. Virtual Reality booths, and superb defensive capabilities." He added nonchalantly, "All we've got to do is steal it."

"We've no Kili to help us this time," Shari pointed out.

"We'll manage."

"No sewers either?" asked Kristas, remembering the fetid underground tunnels they had walked through on Pasiphae. "No armed guards? No treacherous politicians?"

Cruse grinned. "You know I can't promise you that, *dreamer.*" Kristas smiled.

"We're glad," said Shari, and Kristas agreed with her. "The System's not our home any more. We could both do with a few surprises."

Cruse shook his head good-naturedly and stroked Doob. "You two are a couple of crazy kids, you know that?" They nodded their agreement.

"Well, come on, then," he sighed, and led the way. "That big old Universe of ours isn't going to wait forever!" He paused and looked at Shari. "You're really sure you want to leave the System for good?"

Shari looked around the apartment which the System had graciously provided for her. Compared to the living quarters of other TerraNovans it was huge. She had her own personal Virtual Reality booth which meant that she could "visit" the wonders of Old Earth whenever she desired; she had been granted carte blanche to travel to any of the System worlds whenever she wanted; she even had two top-of-the-range ServoRobots to attend to her every whim.

It was a life of luxury and privilege which many on TerraNova would have killed for; a safe and easy life of comfort and boring predictability.

And outside the System there was only danger and uncertainty and the wonder of the new.

"To hell with the System," she said, walking through the door. "C'mon Cruse, there's a whole Universe waiting for us out there..."